SEA OF TROUBLE

SHAPE UP OR SHIFT OUT BOOK 3

MANDY ROSKO

SEA OF TROUBLE

SHAPE UP OR SHIFT OUT BOOK 3

Who wouldn't want to accept a free cruise? Especially if that means a chance at meeting your true fated mate?

Bill isn't over his ex. He left her high and dry half a year ago, but it's time he moves on. He's a Grizzly bear shifter with cybernetic enhancements and a dark past. He's not sure what kind of woman can learn to love a man like that. Ray hates water and boats, but this red panda shifter is going to suck it up and get on board because it's been far too long since she's dated anyone—ever since her ex completely ghosted her—and she's got a good feeling about this matchmaking cruise.

All hopes are dashed, though, when the two exes end up assigned to the same room... and there are no other cabins available!

Can Ray and Bill reunite? Or will their sea of troubles be too much to sail through?

CHAPTER
ONE

WHEN ESME TOLD RAY THAT SHE WAS GIVING HER A GIFT, something to help her relax, this was definitely not what Ray had in mind.

She hated the water, but it was a free cruise. Her flight to Miami had been paid for. The cruise itself was paid for, and that included food and onboard entertainment.

The only thing Ray had to deal with on her own was buying fancy drinks or shopping, and with all the cash she'd been saving, it had seemed like an easy enough choice at the time.

Not to mention, it was a chance to meet her mate

How could she say no to all of that?

Now, she couldn't believe she was doing this.

Ray held her bag closer to herself. She'd been chatting with some of the other passengers before it was their turn to walk on board the ship itself. Gia, a nice enough bear shifter, had taken her mind off of what she was about to do, but now that she was walking onto the ship, so many people crowded around her in the tunnel, eager, chatting, luggage rolling...

1

It was starting to sink in.

Ray really didn't need to be thinking about the word *sink* while she was boarding a luxury cruise liner.

She passed multiple beautiful women in uniforms lining the walls, smiling and offering assistance, and answering questions to anyone who needed it.

Ray tried not to look at any of them. She tried not looking outside and towards the water, either.

She wasn't even on the boat yet, and she already wanted off it.

She hated the water. Ray was a red panda shifter, not a Goddamn dolphin.

Why the hell did she ever let Esme convince her it was a good idea to go on a trip like this?

The walk seemed to take forever, and Ray really wished she hadn't lost her new friend Gia in the crowd. She could use someone to take her mind off this all over again.

After walking through the tunnel thing and finally getting onto the ship itself, Ray stopped walking.

It was probably a little rude, and people needed to maneuver around her, but she needed a second to breathe.

The floor beneath her feet was shockingly sturdy.

Well, it *was* a cruise ship. And a good one, too.

For some reason, Ray was expecting to get onto the boat and feel the ocean beneath her, rocking and constantly moving, reminding her of all the creatures beneath the surface she couldn't see—both beautiful and deadly.

She kind of could feel that the ground wasn't exactly *solid*, but not at all like it had been on the little fishing boat she'd been on as a kid. That one had been tiny and completely unstable, and she couldn't get off it quick enough.

This one, though; was it possible it would be okay?

She rolled her shoulders and ignored the curious and irritated looks of the other passengers who passed by her.

She smiled apologetically at them but couldn't bring herself to take any steps out of the way as they passed her by. Not even to the ones who were, not so quietly, whispering about how rude she was.

Whatever.

Ray knelt down, opened her satchel, and yanked out her phone.

She immediately searched for the email she'd saved.

It was in the folder where she'd also put her tickets for this damn thing.

Esme was an... interesting woman, to say the least.

Ray had met her by chance. The woman claimed to be a matchmaker and had asked Ray if she was looking for love. Ray answered yes, of course. Who wasn't? Then, somehow, that petite and understated woman made Ray sing like a songbird desperate for food, pulling out her entire life story, hopes, and dreams.

Also, her regrets and disappointments.

Honestly, it was way too much TMI for anyone to reveal to a complete stranger.

No matter how helpful she claimed to be.

But, what was done, was done.

Ray re-read the email for what had to be the ten-thousandth time. She was already on the damn boat, so it wasn't like she needed to keep convincing herself. Still, she reread it, just to steady her heart that was currently trying to bust through her skin.

Darling,

I know you mentioned you don't like the water, but a little sea air is good for the soul. Don't worry. It's a fine ship, and you'll barely notice you're on the water when you get there. I promise everything you've been waiting for will be on that cruise.

Hugs and kisses, and don't be so paranoid. Have lots of fun. You deserve to wear a bikini and look fabulous for your mate.

Attached were the tickets for the cruise and the airplane.

It was strange how getting on the plane had been easier than getting into the damn ship. For most people, it would have been the other way around, but Ray had a thing about water.

Ray sighed. What could she do? If Esme insisted this was where Ray needed to be to get closer to her goals, then she'd be a complete idiot to say no. The woman had a reputation for an uncanny ability to find shifters' true mates.

It was like some sort of cosmic gift. In a world where shifters existed, the lady who knew love inside and out was still the reigning queen.

So, yeah, Ray came.

"Miss? Are you all right?"

Ray startled, looking up at the... deckhand? Employee? Whatever, a guy who wore the ship's colors and logo, so must work there. He was young and a little skinny and looked a little unsure whether or not he should even be talking to her.

Or maybe he was unsure about whether or not he needed to call medical services.

"Do you need help finding where you're going? If you take these elevators up, you'll find the deck, where the embarkation party will be starting soon. If you want to go to your room, I can let you know which of the other elevators to take."

Ray glanced around and realized she'd been standing in the atrium so long that there were no longer throngs of people boarding. The crew was closing the big doors, and only a few other guests dotted the area.

Passengers were likely not meant to stand around and just watch them.

"Sorry, no, I was just checking my emails. I'll get going."

The kid smiled at her, nodding. "If I may recommend, a lot of people need some time to get used to the ship. It's not uncommon to spend a day by the pool with a few drinks with your friends."

She hadn't brought any friends with her, a topic she'd covered with the woman, Gia, she'd met before boarding. It was okay, though. A mimosa and working on her next project by the pool while waiting for Mr. Right to finally show up sounded amazing.

Doing her hair and makeup so she would look fetching from a distance seemed suddenly important.

"Thank you so much for that. You're right. Uh"—she showed him her ticket with her room number—"where do I go, just down this big hall?"

"Yes, down this hall." Luckily, the kid didn't look at her like she was an idiot for asking what should have been obvious as he pointed the way with his whole hand. "It will get a little louder with the other passengers, and it will lead you right to the shops and restaurants. Everything will be clearly marked and color coded. If you lose your way, please don't hesitate to let a member of staff know, and we'll be happy to assist you."

Damn, these guys were really chipper.

They must be paid well.

Or maybe working on a cruise liner on the ocean in mostly beautiful weather was enough to put anyone in a good mood.

It probably didn't hurt that they had the chance of hooking up with guests that would never be seen again.

Either way, Ray followed his directions, and the kid had been right. It was idiot-proof. The long corridor led away from the boat she'd come in on, and it definitely got louder as she reached the end.

Double doors opened easily for her, leading her into the shopping area of the ship, where so many passengers browsed the overpriced shops on board.

She clutched her bag closer to herself.

If anyone thought she was strange for holding tightly to an oversized messenger bag instead of a cute little colorful purse, no one looked at her funny for it.

But walking by all the shops, seeing the hats, the shoes, the too-expensive bathing suits, and flip flops—and yes, even the purses—made her think about all the reasons she needed to buy one.

She was on vacation, after all, and it wasn't like she'd paid for the cruise itself, so maybe she could justify spoiling herself...

No. You're already on vacation. That's enough indulgence. You don't need to buy stuff that you'll never use again once you're off the ship.

She sighed, turning away from the temptations of the shops and jumping onto the elevator.

She didn't realize it was already heading up to the deck, not down toward the rooms, until it started moving. When the doors opened on deck, she couldn't help but step out, lured by the enticing smell of the food stands.

More guests sat in chairs around the food stands and pool, chatting with easy smiles and bright laughter over even brighter-colored drinks and amazing-smelling food.

Ray's mouth immediately watered as her nose picked

up on the smells of pork and chicken. She also detected hints of a few different somethings that were sugary and sweet.

God, one couple over there was eating chickens and waffles.

She wanted that *so* bad.

Later. She was hungry now, but she needed to get to her room.

Then find out what sort of salads were on the menu.

Ray was proud of herself that she didn't need to ask for assistance to find her room. She found a touch screen map of the boat that made it easy to figure out where to go, and everything *was* color-coded like the kid had said.

She almost felt like she was inside a mall.

She hopped back on the elevator—going *down* this time —and hit her floor number.

Walking down the hall toward her room, she now felt the distinct hotel vibe.

That changed when she found her room and opened the door with the keycard they'd given to her when she boarded the ship.

Stepping into her room, the first thing she took in was the blue ocean through the veranda door.

It stole her breath away. Terrified and impressed her at the same time.

Now that she was safely inside her room, she could almost admit that it was kind of calming to look at.

There was one decent-sized bed, but Ray barely saw it or anything else in the room as she set her bag down and moved out to the veranda.

It was a tiny balcony, which she was prepared for from her research on cruises. The ships liked to pack as many people on as they could. Besides, oversized balconies for every room wouldn't look so great, and part of the draw of the cruises were always those air shots from the commercials, showing off the beauty and majesty of the ships themselves.

Couldn't clutter that up with a big balcony, after all.

She didn't mind. Ray knew she wasn't going to spend much of her time in her room anyway, and what time she did spend there would be sleeping, showering, and working at the little desk.

If she wanted to enjoy the view, she could go up to the top deck.

Still, this was nice. Her room faced out to sea, but the ship was still docked. They hadn't taken off yet.

This was actually kind of nice. Nothing scary about it at all.

The door behind her clicked.

Ray whirled around, thinking perhaps she'd left it ajar, and it had just swung open.

The tall man standing there, taking up most of the doorway, was not what she expected.

He didn't expect to see her either, with the way his green eyes flew wide and how he dropped his duffle bag at his feet, clearly in shock.

The strangest thing about it was the fact that the man —one of probably a thousand passengers on the ship— wasn't a stranger.

He was someone she knew. Someone she hadn't seen in months. A man who vanished like a ghost.

Now, suddenly right there. On her luxurious cruise vacation.

Her ex-boyfriend.

"Ray?"

She couldn't move. "Uh, hi Bill."

CHAPTER

TWO

Ray blinked a few times, half expecting Bill to disappear, just the way he'd done six months ago.

Vanished. Without a trace. Ghosting her on all apps for weeks after telling her—through a text!—that it was over.

Leaving her heartbroken.

Then furious.

Bill looked a little... different. She'd never seen him dressed so... casual before. When they'd dated, he usually wore a dark suit of some kind, explaining that it was part of his job in security. When he dressed down for dates, it was in dark jeans and a leather jacket over a black T-shirt.

Now, he wore navy shorts and a white button-up with grey boat shoes, and damn if they weren't flattering on him. Of course they were. Because everything was.

He changed his hair, too. Now, it was just long enough that she would have been able to grab a handful of those brown tresses in bed. Before, his hair was always buzzed short.

Ray had always thought he would look good with longer hair, and he did.

The dirty bastard.

The day all of his stuff disappeared from her apartment, she'd wanted to call the cops and report him missing. She would have if he hadn't sent the text in time.

It wasn't a long message. Nothing drawn-out or fancy, but it didn't need to be for her to get the point.

It's not working out.

I need to leave.

I hope you have a good life.

In an instant, the betrayal of getting dumped—by a fucking text of all things—and treated like the two years they'd had were nothing, came flooding back.

"You're in the wrong room," she snapped.

He looked down at his key card, then at the door.

Then back at her. "I don't think I am."

No way. "Bill."

He turned the card so she could read the number on it. He also opened the door wide enough that she could see the number on her door matched.

What?

Fuck. Maybe she was the one in the wrong room.

Sometimes ones and sevens could look a little alike.

"Wait a minute." She scrambled to find her keycard again, pulling it out to have a look.

Nope.

The number on her card was the same as Bill's. The same as what was on the door.

"No, that's not..." She pulled out her phone, desperately clicking to the folder where her ticket was.

Her fingers trembled as she searched for it.

There it was... and the number on the ticket was the same one on her keycard and door.

"Okay," she said, breathing deeply, fighting for calm,

desperately trying to not yell at him, to screech at him to get the hell out and stay the hell away from her.

Serenity now. Serenity now.

"This is clearly a mistake," she said. "We need to find someone and figure out where you're supposed to go."

"Here," Bill replied matter-of-factly. "I'm supposed to be here."

"This is *my* room," Ray snapped. "I'm here with someone."

The lie slipped off her tongue easily. She didn't want Bill to know she was there by herself, that she'd come because she'd been pathetically desperate for Esme to set her up with her true love.

Her fated mate.

She couldn't believe how dumb she'd been to actually believe at one time that Bill was her fated mate. Shifters were supposed to have some special sense that would tell them when they met their fated mate, but her red panda was clearly defective. She'd submit herself to scientific study if she could, but she didn't know of any people researching why a red panda could wrongly identify someone as a fated mate when they really *weren't*.

A fated mate would have never done to Ray what Bill had.

Now Ray didn't feel that love for him. That swoony *fated mates* call.

Only rage. Anger. Hatred.

Fury.

And none of that was at all because she'd missed this stupid, ignorant, selfish asshole either.

"You should go to the front desk, concierge, customer service, whatever, and tell them there's been a mistake. You're not staying here."

Bill stared at her for what felt like the longest minute of her life. His lips thinned, lips she'd once ached to kiss at the end of the day. He hadn't shaved in a couple of days, which always made him look so much more handsome.

Fuck, stop thinking about how handsome he is! He was a fucking asshole, and he didn't deserve to have her think nice things about him.

Bill leaned down and grabbed the handles of his duffle, slinging it over his shoulder and stepping back. "Sorry for the intrusion."

"Right, no problem," she said, even though it felt like a *very big* problem.

Ray felt like she held her breath when he turned around and quietly shut the door behind him, leaving her alone to exhale hard.

Fuck if her legs didn't itch to chase him down, tackle him to the ground and demand some answers.

Like where the fuck he'd been, why had he left, and what she'd done wrong to make him go.

Nope. Not gonna debase herself like that. Ray was a new woman and what he did was not her business. It was all in the past.

She couldn't be on this amazing cruise, trying to meet her *true* fated mate, just to still be hung up and angry about her ex.

That would definitely make for terrible first impressions.

Unless...

There was no way.

Could Esme...?

No.

Ray gripped her phone tight enough that she risked breaking the stupid thing as she pulled up Esme's number.

She called it four times in a row. No answer each time, but she left a voice mail on the last try.

"Esme, it's Ray, the red panda. Do me a huge favor, and please call me back as soon as you can. It's important, and I need to talk to you. Right away. Seriously."

She debated with herself saying this next part, but knowing voice mails couldn't last forever, she spit out the next part.

"Bill is here. Did you do this? You didn't, right? Because he can't be—"

The phone beeped and cut off her message before she could finish.

Whatever. Ray supposed she got through the main part of her message.

Bill was here. He wasn't supposed to be. Right?

He couldn't be the one Esme was trying to set her up with, right?

Ray was going to die if that was the case.

She went to the phone next to the bed and hit the button for reception. The man confirmed her room number, and then she asked if he noticed a tall man with brown hair and green eyes asking about her room.

"Oh, yes, I see someone with that description speaking to another agent. He's wearing navy khaki shorts and a white shirt?"

"Yeah, that's him. Are you giving him another room?"

"I... I don't know, ma'am. I'm not at his... well, let me go see."

"It's a mistake. He's not supposed to be here," Ray said, though she was pretty sure the guy on the phone couldn't hear her anymore since he went to check in on his co-worker with Bill.

Ray couldn't hear a damn thing, but she could already

picture what was happening down there. They were talking to each other. Talking to Bill, and talking about her, the crazy lady who was checking in to make sure they were all doing their jobs.

When the receptionist came back, he sounded apologetic.

"I am sorry, but it appears when you booked the room—"

"I didn't book the room," Ray corrected. "A friend of mine did."

"I understand, miss, but when the room was booked, it was booked for two."

Her stomach dropped.

She forced herself to relax. "Okay, no problem. Can you give him another room? I'll pay any fees for the last-minute changes if he won't."

"It's not so simple as that, I'm afraid."

Ray's hand clenched tightly around the phone receiver. She struggled to get the words out through her teeth. "Why not?"

"Every room has been booked up, even our suits. There is nowhere else. If there was a mistake where you both booked your room—"

"We didn't book the room. I mean, I don't know if he did, but my friend booked this room for me. Esme Baer."

Ray didn't like name-dropping like that, but things were dire. It might be the only way she could kick something into gear.

It didn't work.

"Then she booked it for the both of you, I'm afraid. Ray Donaldson and William O'Bourne are booked to this room."

God, *no*.

This was a fucking disaster.

Ray had to take a couple of deep breaths. Her ears were ringing, and suddenly the room she was in seemed *so* small, the bed too tiny, and an inadequate amount of air around her despite the fact that her veranda door was still open.

"Uh, okay, uh, this might have been a mistake."

Esme, please don't let this be true. Why would you do this to me?

"I'm so sorry," said the receptionist, who was clearly uncomfortable and had nothing to offer and just wanted to get off the phone

But then an olive branch was offered.

"Sometimes guests leave early. Business or family events come up. People get sick. We'll put a note here, and if a room becomes vacant, we will move one of you into it."

That was something.

Ray told herself not to panic. This could be fine. "How long does it usually take for someone to leave the boat?"

"The earliest we've had was the same day, but on average, a day or two. Someone always has to leave for one reason or another."

Ray thought about it, and it made sense. A cruise ship with this many guests on it, some who probably ran their own businesses or had families to take care of at home, based on the numbers alone, yeah, someone, or a couple of someones, would eventually have to leave early.

"We're so sorry again for the inconvenience," said the receptionist, who then proceeded to hum and haw about what they could possibly offer Ray for compensation for the mistake.

Which was difficult considering almost everything was already paid for by someone else.

Esme getting a discount on future cruises wouldn't help Ray's situation, after all.

But then the receptionist brought on his manager, who clicked around on the computer, refusing to let Ray hang up even when she was feeling kind of better about the whole thing and just wanted to flee the room before Bill returned.

Ray's interest was piqued when they offered her a free voucher for a thousand dollars to spend in any of the shops and spas on board the ship.

She immediately remembered the cute purses, shoes, and bathing suites she's seen in the shops, and how she'd wanted to doll herself up for when she met her true mate onboard.

Because there was no way that Bill *was who Esme was setting her up with.*

In the end, she accepted the offer because what other choice was there?

She waited on the manager to confirm her email address, name, and date of birth before loading the voucher onto the account she apparently already had.

"It's all there. You just have to use your keycard to access it."

"Won't Bill have access to the same money?" she asked.

"He is being compensated separately, and his card has a different code from yours. I assure you, he does not have access to your gifts."

Ray figured it was a system they had so parents who came with kids during the family cruises wouldn't have to worry about little Timmy or Amy spending any money that wasn't loaded on their own room cards.

Whatever. Ray was suddenly feeling much happier about this whole thing.

She had to be around the man who'd walked out on her and broken her heart, but at least she was going to get a shopping spree out of it.

Ray thanked the manager on the phone, patiently answered the automatic questionnaire about the level of service, and gave five stars to everything, then quickly hung up.

She looked at the bed and around the room.

There wasn't anywhere else to sleep except on the floor.

She pulled down the comforter and made sure to set her bag on top of the bed, claiming her space.

There were multiple pillows. She spared one for the floor. There were no extra blankets or sheets, but a housekeeper with a full cart down the hall handed over extra sheets and blankets.

It took Ray all of two minutes to have a nice little spot set up on the floor for Bill.

And he was lucky she was bothering with doing that much for him.

For now, after setting a couple of her outfits on the bed, she grabbed her work bag and decided to enjoy some of the shopping and pampering that was promised by the cruise staff.

Mind made up, Ray went to the shops to buy something cute and schedule an appointment to get her nails done.

She was here to meet her mate, after all.

Couldn't get that done while thinking of her asshole ex.

CHAPTER

THREE

This was a fucking disaster.

Bill spent more time than he meant to at the front desk, desperately trying to figure out if there was anywhere else he could stay.

He even offered to bunk in with some of the crew, but not even any of those cabins were available.

He could tell that was a lie.

It wasn't the Grizzly bear inside him that picked up on it, either.

His implants—the chips in his brain and his eyes—picked up on that.

He was pretty good at telling when people were lying to him nowadays, and he knew they just didn't want him in employee-only areas.

It was irritating, but he supposed it made sense.

But it didn't help his problem any.

Ray is here. Ray was in the same room as he was.

While the managers and guest agents apologized profusely for the mix-up and loaded him up with free money to spend at the bars and shops, all he could think about was how Goddamn gorgeous Ray's dark red hair looked tumbling around her shoulders. How he could almost count the freckles on those same shoulders thanks to the thin straps on her summer dress.

She'd always been a little on the short side, something he attributed to her animal shape being so small, but in that moment, with the ocean behind her, lighting her up, she just seemed so much... more.

Bill closed his eyes, elbow on the counter, fingers pressing on his temple while the manager typed furiously on the computer, trying to set up something that would make this whole thing a lot less miserable for him.

They couldn't do shit other than get Bill into a new room, but even if they did, Bill wasn't blind.

Esme had done this shit on purpose.

That woman had a reputation, and Bill knew of it. He'd done his homework on the woman.

A lot of it.

It used to be his job to look into people, so it wasn't difficult.

Esme Baer didn't make mistakes, and she didn't do anything unless it was a means to an end. She didn't go out of her way to set people up with their exes unless she was sure there was some unfinished business going on, and that was clearly what this was.

She had a scary accurate track record of setting people up with their fated mates. It was freaky. He'd even asked around, put out feelers, so he could meet a few of them and find out if they really were happily mated.

They were.

Was it possible that some couples didn't work out? Sure, but no one was talking about it, and it wasn't like there was a record anywhere of that. And he knew well enough that if someone didn't want to be found, he sure as fuck wasn't going to bother them because that was opening up a whole other can of worms.

He was one of those people. He didn't want anyone to know where he was unless he wanted it, and God help anyone who tried finding him when he didn't want to be.

Every single couple he spoke to—or the ones he heard about and then looked up on social media—was perfectly happy and content with their mates. All gave Esme the sort of rave reviews that big-name companies couldn't even pay for.

Was this a sign? It had to be, right?

Back when it happened six months ago, he'd hated leaving Ray.

But he'd had to. There was no choice.

Now she was here. Because of Esme.

Bill was suddenly regretting that he'd been so honest with Esme when he'd met her at a party he was working security for.

The woman had been so charismatic he couldn't help but talk to her, even though she seemed unusually interested in him and his love life.

He'd chalked it up to a natural matchmaker's curiosity. She'd been *very* interested in hearing about his ex and definitely hadn't accepted his vague excuses for why he'd left Ray after two years of dating bliss.

When he'd left, Bill fully expected to never see Ray again. Sure, he'd gone back to the dating scene, but only because loneliness could still hit a cyborg's brain. Plus, it had been long enough that he was mostly sure his old boss wouldn't be an issue.

He just didn't expect Esme to set him up with *Ray* after all was said and done.

In the end, there was fuck all he could do but hope that someone got seasick or had some work emergency they needed to leave the ship for. In the meantime, regardless of what Esme was trying to do, Bill couldn't go back to that room.

Ray *hated* him.

Bill didn't blame her for it, either.

He thanked them when the guest relations manager informed him that his voucher was loaded on his card. He left, still feeling defeated, despite getting to spend as much as he wanted on booze for the night without having to worry about his finances.

Because God knew he wanted to blow his life savings on hard liquor right about now.

He pulled his duffel bag tighter over his shoulder and reached for his phone to try calling Esme.

He called twice, and there was no answer, so he was pretty sure that meant either Esme was too busy to talk, or Bill was being intentionally ignored.

Esme had to know he'd want to complain about this.

Six months.

He'd backed off from his damn job, left his girlfriend of two years, and after six months of being lonely as fuck, this happened.

What the fuck was his life right now?

He passed by multiple happy couples. He didn't know who came onto the cruise together and who was there just for the chance to meet their fated mates. It didn't matter. All the smiles, the staring into each other's eyes and hand-holding that was going on around him was enough to make his guts clench up, and his chest ache.

Thankfully, it was easy enough to find one of the many onboard bars that served shifter-strength drinks.

Most of the tables were small, with only two seats, but the bar itself was long and open and comforting to sit at.

The bartender was overly cheerful, there was some dancing, and the music wasn't too loud yet. Bill figured that would change when the sun went down.

The bartender accepted Bill's card, commented how it was his lucky day to have such a balance on it, but then stopped smiling when Bill growled at him.

The guy handed over the drink, then quickly went off to see to the other patrons who would be more appreciative of his smiles and chatter.

Bill didn't know what sort of shifter that guy was, but he was willing to bet it was one of the smaller species. It was difficult for Bill to tell for sure, since he couldn't pick up on any particular scents around him. Too many people, too many perfumes.

Bill, however, was a Grizzly. Most people could sense the larger shifters.

Which was why most of them scrambled the fuck away when one was in a bad mood, as he was now.

He couldn't give off too much of a *fuck you* vibe, however. He needed that bartender to keep his drink filled.

The guy eventually found his balls and came back, refilling Bill's drinks and swiping his card. Eventually, Bill took him up on his offer for food, but only because he needed something to do other than wallow.

Ray is here. Ray. Is. Here. They were sharing a room, and she was fucking gorgeous.

Looked a little different, though. Had she cut her hair? It seemed a touch shorter, but there was something else he couldn't entirely place.

Whatever. Not his problem. Ray wasn't his business anymore.

Esme was never wrong? Fuck off with that. Everyone was wrong sometimes, and this was one of those times for Esme. Clearly.

He checked his phone, searching for any messages from the matchmaker.

There were none. *Of course not.*

He finished his club sandwich and fries, which were shockingly good. Bill didn't take any more booze, though, opting for water at this point because, fuck, even though he was a bear and could hold his alcohol, this cruise didn't mess around when it came to the strength of shifter drinks.

And the fact that he might have to sleep in the same room as the former love of his life made him realize that he might not want to show up completely smashed.

The hours passed. He still couldn't bring himself to leave the bar.

More people showed up, more dancing, the music grew louder, and his head was really starting to hurt.

The bartender was busy, which was probably great for his tips, but as the time dragged on, he was staring at Bill with more pity in his eyes than fear.

Fuck.

It was getting a little too busy in there. Bill needed to go.

He fished out his wallet and fumbled for a twenty. He held it up so the bartender could see it and put it on the counter for him.

Bill was already turning to get the hell out of there.

The dancing couples were really starting to piss him off, and he honestly didn't know how much more of this he was supposed to take.

The further away he walked, the more muted the sounds became, but they were still noticeable. There was no forgetting he was on a ship bobbing on the ocean, full of people who were having a great time.

Neon lights had been turned on around the pool for guests who enjoyed a nighttime swim. Bill tried to ignore all of them as he wandered around the ship.

More than once, he caught the eye of a woman looking his way.

Clients of Esme's, wondering if he was their mate? Possibly.

Random cruise-goers looking for a random hookup? Also possible.

He could tell one woman, in particular, watched him curiously. She had flowing dark hair, tanned skin, and a willowy frame.

She was taller than Ray, who'd always been a little self-conscious about her height.

She'd never needed to be. Bill had always loved her just the way she was.

While he thought of his ex, the strange woman kept right on watching him.

Why shouldn't she?

And why shouldn't he smile back? Approach her and ask her how she's doing this evening? She's young, pretty, and clearly interested, so why not? Bill *was* on the ship to find someone.

He was there to forget about the woman he was currently sharing a room with and find the person he would love and care for, for the rest of his life.

Why not see if it could be someone else?

He dismissed the thought quickly.

It wasn't someone else. That was the fucking problem.

From the corner of his eye, he saw the woman walking toward him, looking hopeful and kind of shy.

He pretended not to see her and darted around a corner, walking quickly away before he let her get her hopes up even more.

He assured himself that if Esme had brought the woman on the ship, then she'd find her match—it just wasn't Bill.

He had to focus on his own problem: he had nowhere to go.

He didn't want to be in any of the nightlife places where people were having a good time on their first night of vacation. He passed a karaoke bar and kept on walking. That would just lead him to more of the same. He was sick of seeing happy couples, and he didn't want any other singles looking his way and wondering if he was the guy they were meant to hook up with.

As he moved further away from the party side of the ship, he saw some signs advertising speed dating and couples trivia.

Christ.

He didn't want to go back to his room in case Ray was there, but he sure as hell couldn't stay out all night either.

He checked his phone for what felt like the tenth time, waiting for some news from the cruise staff—letting him know another room had been secured for him—or an update from Esme.

He received neither.

Bill thought he should maybe leave the damn boat himself.

He moved up to the deck, growling under his breath at the sight of happy couples in their bathing suits cuddling up. He went to the railing and sighed, staring off into the horizon.

It was dark out now, but in the distance, he could see the lights from Miami, where he'd boarded.

He got the feeling that unless someone was dying or there was an actual emergency, there wouldn't be a way for him to leave the ship that night.

His only reason for needing a hasty exit was that he was a miserable bastard, and that wasn't enough to make the staff want to take his ass off the ship.

His phone buzzed.

Bill nearly dropped it, trying to yank it from his pocket to read the message.

It was from Esme.

Fucking finally.

Bill held his breath, reading the response to his many, many texts.

The message was short and sweet, just like the sender:

Everything you need is on that boat, darling. Relax and enjoy.

He waited for the three little dots to appear, something to show she had more for him than that.

Nothing came.

Bill almost tossed his phone out to sea in frustration because what the fuck was she thinking?

He had to stop himself, more than once, before he shot off a reply to her that he knew he'd regret later when he was more sober.

Leave it alone. At least for a little while.

The most important thing was figuring out what the fuck he was doing for the night because the staff of this damn boat were not getting back to him.

Maybe he *should* ask for a shuttle back to Miami.

They weren't *that* far away from the coast yet.

Fuck. He was tired and a little drunk.

The bear that had been locked away grumbled and growled a little, but it stayed contently inside.

The wires in his head were pleasantly screwy, and he felt that side of his brain—with the mechanical implants—shut down just enough that he almost felt...

Normal?

The things around him weren't as sharp and detailed as he was used to them being since he'd been worked on.

Since his former boss had tried to lobotomize him with too many cyborg chips.

I just want to go to bed.

On his first night of vacation, he should have been mingling, keeping an eye out for his fated mate, and actually enjoying himself. Alas, Esme had put him in a situation where his ex was in his room, so pissed at him she could hardly stand to see him.

Well, he supposed that was just too damn bad for Ray.

He'd given her enough time to get settled with the idea of bunking with him. He was done hiding from her. It was time he got his beauty rest.

He went back to his room.

Their room.

His card still worked. He supposed that was a good sign.

Booked up or not, if Ray had so much as suggested she didn't feel safe with Bill in her room, he figured his keycards would have been reset to prevent him from getting in pretty quickly.

The door opened smoothly, which meant the bolt hadn't been put into place from the inside either.

Another good sign.

Stepping back into the room, he knew immediately she wasn't inside.

Her scent was there, but only faintly. She smelled like cinnamon. Nutmeg. Freshly baked bread.

Delicious.

He'd never told her that. He didn't think she would appreciate it if he told her how she smelled like all of his favorite baking stuff, but it was true then, and it was true now. Her scent hadn't changed, and it just gave him a big craving for some of Ray's sweet pie.

Christ, what the hell was he even thinking?

He let the door close behind him and stripped out of his shoes, shirt, and pants as he shuffled to the bed, definitely choosing to not think about the fact that she was probably out there with another male.

Smiling. Flirting. Drinking.

There was a good chance she might not even come back to the room that night.

That made his stomach clench up. Bill yanked the covers over his head, desperate to drown everything out while not grinding his teeth into a fine powder.

Esme was wrong. She was wrong. So, so wrong.

If Ray had been the right woman for him that whole time, there was no way he would have been stupid enough to walk away from her. No way he would have let himself make that kind of mistake.

No way he could still be fucking it up by thinking of how plump Ray's lower lip looked, how the ocean sun behind her shone nicely on her freckled shoulders and made her hair seem to glow around her.

Ray deserved better than him anyway.

But if he saw her again and she so much as hinted that any male on board the ship wasn't treating her right, Bill was going to find that guy and beat the piss out of him.

CHAPTER

FOUR

It was *waaaay* after midnight by the time Ray finally stumbled down the hall to her room.

She even managed to stop thinking about how she was cruising along on the open water, away from Miami and towards the Cayman Islands.

It turned out none of that bothered her when she was pleasantly tipsy off of all the ship's colorful drinks and then the pampering she'd had courtesy of the thousand-dollar voucher.

She'd met up with Gia during the sail-away party and drank and danced with her until the woman excused herself to go to dinner.

Ray refused to go to her assigned restaurant for the evening. No way she was going to sit at a table across from Bill, no matter how good the lobster bisque might be.

She almost tried to convince Gia to stay with her at the party, but Ray had felt bad about that. If Gia was on the ship, she was likely looking for her fated mate. Esme had invited so many singles on board so she could pair them up, from what Ray understood. There were also many couples Esme had previously matched, there for a romantic vacation.

And then there was Ray and Bill, bitter exes. Assigned a room together because... why?

Not that Ray shared any of that with Gia. The woman didn't need to be burdened with the woes of a near-stranger.

So Gia went off for dinner, and Ray found a quick-service stand and ordered a grilled chicken salad before she went back to the spa to ask if they could fit her in for *anything and everything.*

She had to wait longer than she would have liked, but they kept her relaxed with cocktail after cocktail—shifter strength, of course.

Then it was down to the clubs for some dancing.

Her mind wandered away from the topic of Bill to think about the other thing she'd spoken with Esme about.

Relatives.

Ray had grown up alone, but Esme had told her that things weren't always as they seemed.

She also told her that there may be more than one surprise on board the cruise.

Were her long-lost relatives on board?

Family that she'd never seen. Sisters she never got to have a relationship with.

She should be looking out for anyone who looked like her, not sipping drinks and dancing it up.

But she was having fun, and Ray desperately needed some fun. That was the best she could come up with for her miserable excuse for a life at the moment.

Ray giggled, brushing her hand over her face and through her hair while returning to her room.

She put in her keycard, the light flashing red and refusing her entry.

Wait, was this her door?

She double-checked the number on the card with the number on the door, but before her eyes could focus, the very clear sound of a deep and pleasured moan floated towards her.

Nope.

Definitely not her room.

Oops.

She backed away from the door, happy for whoever was inside. She grinned at the closed door and waved. "Have fun," she said softly, turning and finding the correct door.

It was three doors down, but Ray definitely passed another room where she could hear the rhythmic motions, grunts, and other sounds that came from sex.

She wasn't happy for the people inside anymore.

Now she was a little jealous.

Fuck. That's not how she wanted to be. She didn't want to be miserable because other people were happy.

She found her door and slid her card in, pushing it open when the tiny light flashed green.

She sighed, kicking off her shoes and dropping her work bag on the floor, suddenly grateful she'd decided not to do any actual shopping just yet since she could barely keep track of her current bag.

It was dark in her room, but as the door shut behind her, Ray stopped herself before she could flick on the light.

The smell... it smelled like crisp, spring air and new grass. That was Bill's scent, strong, letting her know he had returned to the room and was in there. Right then.

Ray held her breath.

He was back. Of course he was back. This was his room, too.

Where the hell else was he supposed to go?

Fuck.

It was bad, but it wasn't the disaster Ray expected it to be.

Maybe all those drinks were relaxing her mind about the whole thing.

She had to pee badly because of them, though, so the bathroom was the first place she went.

The damn light nearly blinded her after two seconds of darkness, but she did her thing, brushed her teeth quickly, and used a makeup remover before she could let being too tired, drunk, and lazy talk her out of performing her nightly routine.

Looking into the mirror, Ray thought she looked pretty damn good, even with squinting eyes from the light and messy hair from a night of dancing.

Would Bill still like how she looked? Did he have any regrets about walking away from her all those months ago?

A petty part of her really hoped he would. She wanted him to know what he'd turned his back on. She wanted him to wish he hadn't done what he did.

She also wanted to know *why* he did it.

Since she wasn't getting that answer tonight, she changed into her pajamas.

Since she'd packed in preparation for finding her fated mate, she'd brought some nice silk sleepwear. A negligee, some sexy bras and panties.

Those were staying folded up. None of that for Bill. She was putting on the cotton lounge pants and T-Shirt.

Especially when she walked across the cabin and saw that he hadn't taken the hint. Instead of taking the floor bed, he was in *her* bed. She sighed, tripping a little over the bedding she'd prepared for him—the ungrateful asshole—and climbed into the other side of the bed.

Her traitor heart ached when she realized what side of the bed he'd picked.

He remembered.

They could be in either of their apartments or staying in some random motel, and the only spot on the bed Ray wanted was the one closest to the bathroom.

She usually woke up in the middle of the night, either desperately thirsty or needing to pee once or twice.

Another weird little quirk of hers that she was self-conscious about.

There had been two men before Bill whom Ray trusted and cared for enough to spend the nights with, and her constantly waking up most nights had been deal-breakers for them.

Because when she woke up, so did they.

A bear shifter could sleep through anything, though, and Bill always claimed to not mind when she woke up to do something. Whether get a drink or go to the bathroom.

He'd promised her he didn't care, and it didn't matter to him which side of the bed he got.

Ray's throat closed up as she watched his chest slowly rise and fall, one arm slung high above his head.

He always slept like that. She'd always thought it was cute.

Did he choose that side of the bed because of her? Or was it a mistake? A coincidence, and he'd climbed to that side without thinking of her at all?

More than likely, she was putting too much thought into it.

But it still did something to her, thinking Bill had done

that small thing for her, even though they hadn't slept together in months.

Ray climbed into bed. She was tired, and she was definitely going to wake up once or twice more after all those drinks she'd had in the clubs, but for now, it didn't matter as she tucked herself in under the covers.

She turned on her side, really looking at Bill.

He looked mostly the same, but maybe he'd been under a lot of stress over the last few months because there were some deeper lines at the corners of his eyes and between his brows. He looked a little older if that could even be possible in six short months.

As if he'd been doing a lot of frowning lately.

It looked bad. Ray was struck by the urge to kiss it away —both the deep lines and whatever it was he'd been worrying about these last six months.

Settling into her fresh pillows was easy. Sleeping was easy. Maybe it was the fact that he smelled so familiar and safe.

Not safe for her heart, though. Not even close. He crushed *that* with his bare hands a long time ago, but Ray was still confident she knew Bill well enough as a person to know that snuggling up next to him wouldn't be a problem.

She did end up waking up only once more that night to use the restroom, but somewhere between the haze of being only half awake, the gentle rocking of the ship itself, the smell of sea air, and the toasty, crazy nest of blankets with a solid warm body...

Yeah, Ray ended up snuggling up to Bill like it was old times.

His arm came around her as if on sleeping instinct. Ray smiled, back in time, six months ago, forgetting all about her heartbreak and his vanishing act as she fell into a comfortable sleep for the first time in months.

CHAPTER

FIVE

Bill scrunched his nose, feeling the sun on his face, and suddenly very aware of the rocking boat, the smell of the ocean outside, the sounds of the water, and more distantly, the rest of the cruise ship itself.

More than that, he felt the warm weight of a comfortable body in his arms.

He cracked his eyes open and looked around. Soft, wavy red hair fanned out across his chest. Ray's hair, her head resting on his chest, slim arm around his middle, while his hand rested on her shoulder.

Just like old times. If it weren't for the smell of the open sea outside, he might've forgotten where he was and maybe thought he was back in time, six months ago.

In their room. Waking up to slow kisses and a few happy cuddles.

Before he'd fucked things up and left.

He brought his hand up, carefully, brushing his fingers through that gorgeous head of red hair like he used to.

Ray must have felt it. She sighed, stretching her body out a little before settling her cheek back against his chest.

She didn't wake up, thankfully. Bill held his breath a little before he was sure of that.

He frantically tried to remember what happened the previous night. He came back to the room a little miserable and drunk, but he was pretty sure Ray had not been with him.

He was definitely sure they didn't have sex. He could feel their clothes were still on.

The more likely explanation was Ray had stumbled back to their room last night and climbed into bed. She'd probably been on her side. She liked being close to the bathroom in case she woke up in the night.

She must have woken up a time or two and stumbled back to bed, too tired to realize what she'd been doing when she curled up against him.

Not that he was complaining.

She smelled amazing.

More importantly, she didn't smell like she'd had other males on her. She had the usual smells of people—men and women—likely from just walking around in the crowds, but not any of the easily-identifiable scents that lingered after sex.

Bill took a breath, forcing himself up and out of bed, moving quietly and carefully. He didn't want to wake her, and thankfully, he didn't.

Normally, she was the one who was easy to wake up, but he could tell she wasn't faking it. Her breathing remained steady and soft while she snuggled up with the pillow he left behind.

He had to look away quickly, ignoring the tugging in his heart as he walked around the bed and...

Nearly tripped over the pillow and sheets that were sitting on the floor.

He stared at it, then at Ray.

He must've missed this when he stumbled in last night, but it was clear Ray had expected him to sleep on the floor.

Yeah right. Nice try.

He picked up the pillow and blankets, setting them onto the nearest chair without much care for them.

Ray might not want anything to do with him, but Bill would be damned if he was going to be sleeping on the floor.

He went to the bathroom, brushed his teeth, showered, dressed, and then quickly checked his phone for messages from Esme or the cruise itself.

Nothing either.

Fuck.

He stepped out of the bathroom. Ray was still sleeping.

Bill grabbed his wallet and decided to be gone from here.

Before he did something stupid like wake Ray up, kiss her senselessly, and tell her about Esme's message.

That maybe this wasn't a mistake.

That was a little too pathetic, and after what he did, he doubted she would believe him.

At least not yet.

No more fucking around. He wasn't going to feel sorry for himself and get drunk tonight.

He needed to talk to Esme. No more texting bullshit.

He walked around until he found the gym. There were a couple of guys there and a few ladies, but it was still early enough that it wasn't crowded.

Bill found a quiet corner and tried his luck again.

He expected to have to call her twice in a row and maybe send her a couple of texts before she took pity on him and picked up, so he was stunned into quiet when she picked up on the second ring.

"Hello, darling!"

"Uh..." Fuck, he couldn't say anything.

"Hello? Bill?"

"Right, sorry. I'm here."

"Good, good," Esme purred, sounding way too pleased with herself. "How was your first night?"

"We didn't have sex, if that's what you're asking."

"But?"

Jesus. "But we slept in the same bed."

"And?"

Christ, really? "I woke up with her... we were cuddling."

"There you go!" Esme sang. "I knew you would take the hint sooner or later."

"Okay, but are you sure about this?"

"I don't make your decisions for you, sweetheart. I don't know what you think this is—"

"Okay, come on. You're supposed to be setting me up with my true fated mate, and I get here, and Ray's in my room, and the entire Goddamn boat is booked up—"

"Excuse me," Esme said, her voice shockingly cold, and it froze Bill from the inside out. "I don't appreciate that tone."

"What? I wasn't—"

"You're overthinking." Her voice became gentle again. "I told you, what you're looking for is closer than you thought, but I can't do the work for you."

"Okay... so what does that mean?"

"My God, you're lucky you're handsome because you're not smarter than the average bear, are you?"

Bill breathed in deep through his nose. "Esme, please..."

"*Fix it*," Esme said, something powerful in her voice.

Powerful, yet gentle, while telling him to stop being a dumbass.

Bill held the phone to his ear, letting her words soak in.

He'd never allowed himself to hope.

When he left his... job, if it could be called that, he'd forced himself to get used to the fact that he was never going to see Ray ever again, and if he did, she wouldn't give him the time of day.

"Are you sure?" he asked, looking around the gym, making sure no one was staring at him.

No one was. They were all focused on the weights, the treadmills, and their bikes.

No one gave a shit about the little crisis he was going through, and that was for the best, especially right now.

"Darling," Gerry said again with a sigh. The tough patience in her voice told him to shut up and listen. "I cannot do everything, you know. I can bring you together, but neither fate nor I can do the work that comes after. You need to make amends for your actions. That part is for you to do."

Bill's throat dried out, like he'd taken in a mouthful of sand.

He nodded before he remembered she couldn't see him. "I understand."

"Good," Esme said, suddenly chipper and bubbly again. "I promise you, it's not all that bad. Your mistakes can be fixed if you work on them."

He scoffed. "I told you what happened. You're sure about that?"

"Bill, I've seen more dire situations work out." Now it was Esme's turn to pause. "For example, recently, I paired an omega from the worst of circumstances with her fated alpha and beta."

Bill frowned. "A... threeway?"

He didn't know Esme did that kind of thing.

"That wasn't the strange thing about it," Esme said. "The clumsy alpha bonked his head and actually lost his memory for a hot minute."

"What?"

"But it worked out in the end, and my darling omega was removed from that horrible place. Believe me, if they could make it work, so can you."

It sounded like there was a lot to that story, but he couldn't concern himself with it. All he needed to take away from the conversation was that he had a chance.

So he was running with that.

"Thank you, Esme."

"You're welcome, now kindly say goodbye so I can get some work done, sweetheart. I have other clients to attend to!"

Bill cleared his throat. "Right, right," he said, suddenly feeling like a complete asshole for blowing up her phone.

He had to remind himself that Esme was doing him a *massive* favor.

"Thanks again, and I'll talk to you later."

"Not too soon, sweetheart," Esme said, that purr back in her voice, as if she knew something important that Bill didn't. "You're going to be busy, aren't you."

Jesus Christ. It wasn't like Bill was some bright-eyed, flowery virgin, or a prude, but there was definitely something about the way she spoke that made his neck and face heat up like nobody's business.

"Yes, Ma'am," he said.

"Don't call me ma'am," Esme warned. "And only call me back when you have happy news for me."

She hung up on him abruptly.

Still a little stunned by the whole thing, Bill waited there a moment after he put his phone away, taking a breath and really letting himself think about what Esme had just said.

Esme had invited him there and put him in a room with Ray.

Intentionally.

Now, if he wanted his mate—which he did—he had to work for it.

He'd not dared to think he could ever have a chance with Ray again, not after what he did, but Esme... well, she didn't say it in so many words, but she basically told him he had a chance.

More than a chance, if he played his cards right.

So he had a new mission.

To fix his fuck-up and convince Ray, his true fated mate, that he wasn't an irredeemable douchebag.

Right. He had to get to work.

The first line of business? Call the front desk and tell them there was no longer a need to move rooms.

He had to do a little convincing, especially after the cruise compensated him and Ray with those vouchers, but he basically said they had made peace with the arrangement and didn't want to lose more time from his vacation by relocating.

"Of course, sir," said the guy on the phone, and Bill definitely detected the sound of a smirk when he said it.

This guy figured Bill and Ray were already sleeping together.

Well, he was kind of right.

Anyway, with that out of the way, it was time to find ways to get Ray to talk to him again.

Esme had put him on a mission, and he wasn't going to fail it.

CHAPTER

SIX

RAY WOKE UP SLOWLY, HER FACE PRESSED INTO THE PILLOWS, A familiar, calming scent washing over her even while the sun stabbed at her eyes.

It was that smell that had her sitting up in a hurry more than the blinding sun in her face or the distant sounds of the cruise ship.

She smelled Bill on these pillows. Bill had been using these pillows, and she was currently cuddled up with these pillows, the same way she'd been cuddled up with Bill just last night.

Oh fuck. Holy shit.

Her face and body burned as she thought of all the ways he, hopefully, wouldn't have noticed when he woke up.

Bill woke up first. If Ray had been all over him still, he definitely would have noticed that.

But he didn't wake her, so there was a chance all was well. Maybe she'd moved away from him in the night and hadn't been spooning him like she was still a love-struck puppy, desperately hoping for some affection from the man who'd thrown her away.

God. Ray closed her eyes, hands over her face, and she fell back against the pillows that smelled so much like Bill.

That smelled like the *both* of them.

She forced herself out of that bed, forced herself to stop thinking about how comforting that smell was, and hopped into the shower to wash it all off her.

No, the smell shouldn't be comforting. It should be a reminder of the man who thought her nothing more than a woman he could toss away. She'd only thought it was comforting because it was familiar, because there was still a part of her that missed him.

While washing her hair, Ray decided that she was woman enough to admit to that.

Having feelings for the guy she'd been hoping would be her true mate, whom she had loved and trusted for so long... it was normal.

Especially when he was right here, in her space.

When she left the shower, Ray did another quick check of her messages.

There was nothing from the front desk, so it was likely that no one was leaving early yet.

There was a message from Gia, however. She said her night ended poorly, but at least breakfast was good, and she was looking forward to the excursions that day. She also sent a photo of her breakfast plate, piled high with scrambled eggs, pancakes, and all kinds of fruits.

And beneath that was a call for Ray to get her ass out of bed and come to enjoy the food because it was apparently to die for.

Ray was so glad she'd met the bear shifter. She didn't know Gia all that well yet, and already Ray felt close to her. Ray barely knew the woman, but it was nice to have someone else to have some fun with. They were both here to meet guys, dance, eat, do their nails, shop, and just enjoy themselves.

When she left the bathroom, she almost didn't notice the pillows and sheets on the chair in the corner.

Bill must have seen the setup this morning and tossed it all there.

Ray knew better than to think he would be making use of that space on the floor until a new room could be found for him.

That was fine. Ray was just going to have to stick to her side of the bed.

Easy peasy. She could definitely do that.

Ray had been so preoccupied with thoughts of Bill that she almost forgot she was on a ship, bobbing around on the open ocean.

Huh. Esme had said her fear of water wouldn't matter when she was finally on the ship.

Maybe it was similar to how some people didn't get airsick on those bigger, commercial airlines.

Either way, Ray found herself relaxing a little as she stood on deck, waiting for her turn to board one of the little tinders taking passengers over to the Cayman Islands.

She almost abandoned her idea to go to shore when she saw how choppy the water was and how the little boats bumped around as they ferried passengers to shore.

But she sucked it up.

She also might have held her breath and held on to the railing for dear life the entire short trip, as well.

Once her feet were on solid land, she felt much better and then spent most of the day doing exactly what she was there to do.

Shopping, picking out a cute scarf with pink, peach, and

soft lavender threads. Another pair of sunglasses never hurt anything. Then there was a cute purse she saw.

Lugging around her huge work bag wasn't always ideal for looking stylish, and despite some setbacks, today was a day when she wanted to look good.

Ray caught the eye of more than one male tourist.

One of the pretty ladies even looked her way, and although Ray was flattered by them, even smiled when a couple of people approached her at different times and asked if she was there with someone, the hateful words that always seemed to come out of her mouth were, "Yes, I am."

Fuck. Fuck. Fuck.

The men who came up to her were always polite enough, smiling, shrugging, though also promising her something more if she wanted to ditch her partner.

She ended up with two phone numbers in her brand-new bag.

She wasn't at all sure how to feel about that.

When she stopped for lunch, she ran into Gia in one of the ladies' rooms. The bear seemed just as upset as Ray was about their romantic situations.

"Guess even when Esme's involved, love doesn't come easy." Gia shrugged

"Love is easy enough," Ray surmised. "I think the problem is all the *shifters* involved. *They're* the ones making it difficult."

"You mean, you and me?" Gia laughed.

Ray ruefully nodded. "Yeah, that is what I mean."

They ended up talking a bit more, and maybe Ray had spilled a little more than she meant to, but she felt a little better in the end.

She went back to the ship after that, figuring she'd had

enough shopping and was tired of turning down would-be suitors.

Maybe a part of her hoped she'd run into Bill, too.

There were still many people around her, some looking at the islands in the distance with her while others walked hand in hand in bikinis, swim shorts, and flip flips, towels slung around shoulders, chatting about the food and the fun.

Having the absolute time of their lives and probably fucking like bunnies.

Ray was just a tiny bit jealous.

She put her arms up onto the railing, contemplating the two numbers in her bag, and thought about the next day, when the boat would be going to the private islands, where shifters went off on their own—non-shifters, humans not in the know went to another—so they could shift freely and run around.

Ray felt a little itchy to change. Being so close to Bill, sleeping next to him...

Cuddling up with him...

Her little red panda wanted out, wanted to cuddle up with her Grizzly, right over his belly, over his heart, like they used to.

Bill used to say she was like a little bear heart, all small, soft, and red. His cuddly little teddy bear.

She'd thought *he* resembled more of a teddy bear, but she understood what he'd been saying back then.

Somehow, they'd managed to fit.

So well.

Why did he leave?

She'd been getting better. If only he wasn't on this damn boat. Ray could almost trick herself into thinking she was entirely over him, and the two phone numbers in her bag wouldn't weigh her down so damn much.

"Hey."

Ray jumped.

Did she just manifest that fucker out of thin air?

"Hi," She pushed back a lock of hair that had come loose from the new clip she'd purchased that day.

Bill leaned against the rail beside her.

Close, but not *too* close. He looked out on the islands.

"Nice view."

"Yes, it is."

Awkward. This was way too awkward, and for the first time in the time she'd known him, she had no idea what to say.

Before, it had always been so easy.

"You look nice."

The wind blew, taking with it the ocean smells and his smells and bringing them right to her nose.

Ray inhaled deeply before she could stop herself.

God, his scent was already so good, and combined with the salty, clean scent of the ocean, it was like adding salted caramel on top of her sweet, vanilla ice cream treat.

Innocently making everything so much better.

Ray looked at him. Really looked.

He looked back.

He was wearing similar clothes from yesterday. He must have walked into a store and told the salesperson to give him whatever beachy clothes he had.

Today his khaki shorts were camel-colored, and his shirt a light blue. He wore the same grey boat shoes, and now he also had a pair of black sunglasses.

She could still make out the muscle beneath his shirt.

She could remember what it had felt like to hold onto him, to feel the power in his body as he slept peacefully.

Her shoulder still burned where he'd curled his arm around her last night.

"Did you ever end up finding your sisters?"

The question brought her back to reality and away from the pleasant, buzzing thoughts of how good-looking he was.

"No. Actually, I spoke to Esme about it. I'd almost had the impression that they could be on board, based on what Esme said. But... well, if you're here then you know Esme, and how cryptic she can be."

He laughed. An honest-to-goodness, *do I ever know it,* laugh. "Yeah, that's Esme, alright."

Ray sighed. "I guess I understand why she's like that. She deals with living, breathing shifters. Ones who don't just do what they're supposed to do, be where they're supposed to be. She probably knows that it will work out if people just do what they're supposed to..."

"But people—shifters—are unpredictable," Bill finished for her.

"Yeah." She tried to smile at him.

His smile was equally strained. "Well, I hope they're here. You deserve it."

"Thanks."

Ray's throat was so dry. She didn't want to talk about this anymore.

Her long-lost family used to be all she could think about until Bill came along and evened her out.

His insistence on taking her out to the movies, or to dinner, or a museum, or walks in the park, anything to remind her there was life in the world other than her search, had been a lifeline for her at times.

And why it hit her so hard when he was suddenly gone without a trace and barely a word.

She had missed him.

And she'd *needed* him.

A sudden thought popped up in Ray's head, something a little naughty, and she thought, why the fuck not?

"You meet anyone on board yet?"

"No," he said, quickly, but not too quickly.

He wasn't embarrassed to admit it. That was interesting.

"I did. I got a few numbers."

It wasn't lost on her the way his hands tightened around the railing of the stupid boat. "Oh yeah?"

"Yeah, but I don't think I'm too interested. They, uh, asked me if I was here with someone and didn't wait for an answer before shoving their cards at me."

A little bit of a lie with some of the truth. That seemed like a good way to get around the fact that she'd told those men she was already with someone.

"Hmm," Bill said, and it was all he said, to Ray's disappointment. "You gonna hit them up?"

He was right here. He was standing right here, and it was so weird having this conversation with him.

"I might, but... I thought it would be weird if you and I were sharing a room. Scents and everything."

"Right," Bill growled.

Ray always thought she would hate this. Part of her wanted to hate it. They weren't together anymore, and Bill was clearly fighting against the whole *woman mine* thing he had flaring through his head.

But this would work out well for Ray if she wanted to keep this going.

"I was thinking, for now, since you and I are sharing a

room and there's not much we can do about it, why not spend that time with each other?"

Bill whipped his head around, looking at her sharply.

He didn't look at her like he thought she was crazy.

He looked at her like he wanted to throw her over his shoulder right now and carry her off.

Ray shrugged, glancing away before he could say anything. "If you're not interested, that's fine, but I figured since we were on this beautiful boat, and Esme is trying to hook us up, we might as well, I don't know, make sure of what we've got until we find who we're looking for."

Ray suddenly felt a little slimy for bringing this up. She didn't actually believe Esme was trying to hook her up with Bill—did she?

It was more complicated than that. Bill had broken her heart. Bill had been the one she'd thought was her fated mate until he vanished on her. She'd wanted to come here to find a new love, and she couldn't accept that Esme wanted her to get back together with her ex, could she?

At first, she'd thought maybe Esme had put them together to make them mend fences. Like, maybe saying that Ray wasn't ready to move on until she'd faced her past and made peace with it.

And now, what was Ray doing? Trying to manipulate her way into her ex's pants so she could have one more go with him.

Bill's eyes changed. They were suddenly glowing golden, and Ray really hoped no one was glancing their way because it would soon be impossible for anyone even passing them by to not notice what was up with his eyes.

"You want me to take you back to our room so I can fuck you?"

He sounded so... possessive. The little hairs on the back of Ray's neck and on her arms stood right up.

She really wished she had another drink in her, because this was getting to be almost too much for her to handle.

"Sure, why not?" She tried to sound casual. "It'll give us something to do to pass the time, other than going into those boring speed dating events."

She'd been looking forward to the speed dating. Until Bill walked into her room.

He kept staring at her. The intensity in his eyes could only be called hunger.

And it was a deep and primal thing that she couldn't ignore now that she saw it.

"I'm ready when you are," was all he said.

Warmth pooled just beneath her belly, which was already twisting itself up into knots.

This was such a bad idea. There were so many reasons why she shouldn't do this.

It would just hurt her again.

Since her horny little brain would only let her think about sex, none of that mattered.

The only thing that mattered was that she tried to look good, cool, and confident, as she smiled at him, swaying her hips maybe a little more than she needed to as she smiled at him, sauntered around him, and walked off toward their room.

She glanced back once just to make sure he was following her.

He definitely was.

CHAPTER

SEVEN

OKAY, THIS WAS DEFINITELY A BETTER STARTING POINT THAN BILL thought he would get.

He followed a few steps behind Ray, watching the gentle sway of his little bear's curvy hips as she moved.

He blinked and forced himself to look away, making sure they were actually heading back to their room.

Not that he thought Ray would lead him off somewhere else, but...

Well, he supposed he'd deserve it if she was setting him up for some embarrassing 'gotcha' moment.

No. They went back to their room. Ray stopped in front of the door, her hand on the key card, hesitating for just a hair of a second before she slid it inside and quickly pulled it back out, opening the door when it unlocked for them.

She glanced back at him, her eyes, more gorgeous than he remembered them being, absolutely dancing. "You coming?"

"Yes," he growled, stepping inside and deciding he was done with waiting.

His hands came around her waist, pulling her close as

he pushed her against the wall, lifting her off her feet so she could more easily wrap her arms around his neck, kissing him deeply.

Her lips were softer than he remembered. They tasted a bit like cherry, and her tongue was almost more eager than his as she opened her mouth and met him halfway.

God, he fucking missed this.

Ray wasn't messing around, either. Her thighs were suddenly up his hips, legs wrapped around him. His cock pulsed between their bodies, and all Bill could think about was how long it had been since he'd last been inside her.

He never thought he would be again.

She was different. She wouldn't have been this forward in the past. Before, she'd waited on him to make almost all the moves or get them most of the way, leaving her the chance to gently follow if she wanted to.

This felt like she was absolutely taking what she wanted, and coming from her, it was surprisingly hot.

Even the feel of her body was a little different. The intensity of the way she clung to him.

It was this place. Had to be. All the horny, pleasantly drunk people walking around, and she'd definitely been to a spa as well. Her skin was baby-soft, and she smelled like something that reminded him of those cucumber masks he'd seen people using on TV.

It was still her, though.

Bill pushed away from the wall. He easily found the bed, setting her on top of it as he pulled off his shirt with some help from her slim fingers.

Even with all the new scents, the changes in both her and him, and the time that had passed since they'd last been together, Ray was exactly the same.

Esme was right again.

Because of course she was.

Ray's hands worked quickly on his belt, pulling his shorts down. He barely had the chance to kick out of his shoes, and he definitely couldn't step out of his khakis before her hands were on his dick and her wet mouth wrapped around it.

Oh. Okay. He didn't think she was *that* eager. Bill figured he would have to go down on her first, in a sort of apology for the way he'd left things before she would even want to touch him like this, but he wasn't about to complain either.

"Baby," he moaned, his hands coming into her red hair. "Fuck."

Suddenly, she pulled back, taking her sweet mouth with her and making Bill feel a sudden rise of panic when she smiled up at him.

"That's all this is, so don't get your hopes up," she said, pulling back and grabbing the hem of her lacy, floral top, pulling it off her body and tossing it on the floor.

Leaving her only in her bra and capris.

With his dick hanging out, hard and throbbing between them, he wanted to get her out of those close right now.

She kept looking at him, something in her whiskey-colored eyes that was... not entirely confidant. Bill got the feeling that was what she was going for. She was trying to be sexy and sure, but she kept looking at him as if...

As if she thought he would leave again.

He felt the desperate clenching in his guts when he caught that from her. It wasn't just her body language. He could almost pick it up in her scent. Her sweat glands had opened up, and he was pretty sure that wasn't entirely due to what they were about to do.

"I'll take care of you," he said, a low, sure rumble in the back of his throat as he stroked her thighs.

Ray swallowed hard, her hands working the button of her pants while he pulled them down her legs.

Fuck. His shorts were still bunched up around his ankles. He kicked them off while pulling her pants and little red panties away.

He held the lacy panties up, looking at them, then at her, and he couldn't help but grin. "This isn't your usual thing."

An embarrassed, red flush crawled up her neck and settled into her cheeks. "I went shopping after you left. Updated some things."

"Some things." Not a question, but his next phrase was. "Will I get to see them?"

Ray raised her chin. "If you're good."

Bill shivered, the bear inside him roaring to life.

"God, I—" He stopped himself, not entirely sure what he would have said.

I missed you? I love you?

Neither were great for him to say right then, and both would definitely ruin the mood.

"You're beautiful," he said, instead, leaning in and kissing Ray's belly, pretending he didn't know how much those simple words embarrassed her.

She'd never been great at taking compliments, and he didn't want to trouble her with thinking she had to say anything back as he kissed his way down, down, down.

Ray gasped, her fingers pushing through his hair and gripping tightly as he lifted one of her legs, putting it up to rest on his back and shoulder while he open-mouth kissed her hot sex.

Her spine arched almost right off the bed. Her gasping breaths took up all the noise in their room.

Bill couldn't hear anything except her as he pushed his

tongue forward. She was wet for him. She smelled so ready that it made the stupid animal side of his brain pace around restlessly inside his head.

It wanted out. It wanted to fuck. To take what was so clearly theirs and what Bill had been so stupid to walk away from.

Even though Ray had invited him back here, and even though she was probably asking for a one-time thing, this wasn't going to be fucking.

He wondered if she knew that as he stroked her trembling legs. The way she thrust against his face was enough to make his cock throb.

God, she tasted fucking great.

"B-Bill," her throat was ragged. "I'm... I'm gonna,"

He pulled back quickly. "Don't you dare."

She shook her head, her hands covering her face, and he knew there was nothing to be done for it. Even though he'd stopped moving, the tension in her body, the tremble that rippled through her made it apparent he'd already pushed her to climax.

He didn't just want her to be gently pushed over that edge, though. He wanted her to sail over it.

Bill cursed, pushing himself back up the bed and adjusting her legs around his waist. He lined himself up, his own body vibrating with what he needed to do as he pushed deep inside her with a heavy groan.

She was so, damn, tight. Better than he remembered. Everything he'd thought about and regretted giving up was all magnified now that he had her again. He couldn't stop moving even if he tried as he slammed inside her.

Ray cried out. Her hands were on his shoulders, her face buried in the crook of his neck and shoulders as her legs tightened around him.

Bill was vaguely aware that she was trying to thrust back against him. Their rhythm was off, but in a gloriously chaotic way. It was beautifully messy and uncoordinated, and he wouldn't have it any other way.

Ray shouted, a little too close to his ear, but he didn't mind as he felt her wet sex tighten even more around him, pulsing, her nails digging into his skin and making him come completely undone.

He came with a shout, hard and heavy, as he fucked into her until there was nothing left for him to give.

He collapsed on top of her, breathless and heavy and...

"Oh fuck," he said.

"What?" Ray asked, sounding sleepy and smiling softly.

"Are you on the pill?"

She snapped her eyes open and stared at him, then looked down between them, as though only remembering there was no condom.

She'd been on birth control when they were together, but that was six months ago, and he didn't know what her routines were anymore.

She exhaled softly. "Yeah, I'm still on it," she said. "But, uh, maybe if we do this again, we remember to put something on you. Just in case."

He nodded. That made sense, and he was a little too happy to hear her say they might be doing this again to let himself panic too much.

"You go it."

"You're heavy."

"I'm comfortable," he retorted, then thought quickly. "You want to take a shower?"

She looked at him again, seemed to think about it, and responded. "Definitely."

EIGHT

RAY WAS A LITTLE EMBARRASSED WITH HERSELF FOR NOT BEING able to last longer.

When she'd invited Bill back to their bedroom to... *to fuck*, the little fantasy she'd created in her mind had set her up to be the sexy, irresistible minx who could go on for hours.

Maybe even outpace Bill entirely, proving to him once and for all what an idiot he'd been for leaving her behind because he could have had something amazing, and now he didn't.

Except, that was totally not how it worked.

Even while Bill turned on the hot water for their shower —which was cramped but could still fit two if you didn't mind the closeness—Ray clenched and unclenched her hands, hating him for still being the confidant one.

For being the one with all the control.

For being the one who left.

And angry with herself for not having a damn ounce of self-control.

Then she was under the warm spray with him, and all

that anger drained away with the water when he kissed her.

They did more kissing under the spray than washing, which was probably bad, but Ray suddenly didn't care. She felt a moment of redemption when, between them, she noticed Bill was getting hard again.

She glanced down, then smiled back up at him, pleased to see that, for once, he looked like he was the one who was struggling to hold it together.

"You don't gotta do nothing," he said a little gruffly.

Right. Even though he definitely wanted her to do something.

Ray wanted to do something, too. She wanted to prove that it had been a mistake for him to leave her behind, that no matter who else he found on this boat, no one was going to come remotely close to her.

No other relationship would give him what they'd had, and he'd been an idiot to walk away.

Which was what she told herself as she sank to her knees and took his cock back into her mouth.

He'd just come, so what she did to him now was a much slower act than what they'd been doing before. There was nothing quick and desperate about this, and the fact that Ray didn't have to worry about being the one to pop off too damn soon made her feel so much braver.

Much more confident as she felt his legs trembling and heard his fist land on the wall.

Bill actually had to hold his hands out on the side of the shower wall just to keep some balance, and damn if that wasn't a turn-on for Ray.

She felt him getting close, pulling back to look up at him, her knees aching a little, but she ignored that as he stared down at her with something akin to amazement on his face.

Which was beyond delightful for her, making him actually lose his stiff composure for once.

His eyes flashed blue. They did that whenever she got under his skin. Instead of his green eyes turning red or gold like was normal for shifters like him, they turned blue.

And that blue was brighter than she could ever remember them being in a long time.

"Are you… are you going to…"

She could let him suffer. She totally could, and would probably even be a little justified in rinsing herself off, exiting the shower, dressing, and walking her happy ass right out of their room so she could spend more time by herself on the ship.

Instead, she slowly stroked the length of his cock, looking up at him and feeling a little mean about it. "Say please."

Bill's eyes popped wider than she'd ever seen them, his nostrils flaring, and again, Ray got that feeling deep inside her that she was finally getting a reaction out of his annoyingly over-calm self.

Her heart hammered as she watched him. She tried to think of what she looked like from his perspective.

On her knees, breasts out and right there, staring up at him with her lips slightly parted only inches away from his cock…

He shuddered, clenching his eyes shut before popping them open again, the blues practically glowing. "Please," he rasped. "Please."

Ray paused for a moment, shocked.

She'd never heard him sound like that before.

Instead of making her feel alive and powerful, it did…

something else. Something she couldn't name, not in real words, but the feeling it invoked within her was to lean forward once more.

The feeling that she needed to give her alpha bear exactly what he wanted because he was straining, and she needed to protect him from that discomfort.

Ray took him back into her mouth. She kept her hands firmly on his firm hips, moving slowly and sweetly, getting into the rhythm of it and enjoying the sounds Bill made for her.

Ray was the one who made him feel this way. He needed to remember that.

He groaned and shuddered, one hand on her shoulder and the other still on the shower wall while she sank her mouth as far down his shaft as she could.

She tried to keep her throat open, tried to take him all the way, but he was big, and his size had never been one she'd managed to deep throat.

Even though she used to practice on him plenty of times in the past.

Ray stopped herself from going down that emotional road. No, memory lane wasn't where she needed to be.

That wasn't what this was about, and she didn't want to get all choked up on something other than his cock.

What they were doing in this room—in this shower— was just two past sexual partners getting out some pent-up tension so they could go about looking for new relation- ships without being distracted by a need to fuck.

Ray finished him off to the best of her ability. She enjoyed the way Bill groaned above her, loved how she was able to bring him such pleasure, and something warmed inside her when he looked down at her, his eyes soft and green again, his lips curled at the side in a sweet smile.

"How was that?"

"Amazing," he said, pulling her up.

He tried to kiss her, but Ray turned away from him suddenly.

"Uh, you sure you want to do that right now?"

"Yes," he said with a low growl that made her heart stop, and then he kissed her.

Deeply.

He wouldn't have done that before. He'd kissed her after she'd gone down on him, but not after she'd swallowed him the way she just had.

Things were definitely different. Something massive had changed between now and the last time she'd seen him.

She didn't entirely know what it was, but she liked it. She liked the way he held her, how his hands strayed down to her ass, gripping her cheeks and pulling her closer still.

Her whole body felt warm, being naked and pressed skin to skin to Bill, as he kissed her more deeply and lovingly than he'd ever kissed her back when they had been together.

Maybe the breakup was actually a net positive for their sex life because, holy shit.

She didn't want to have sex again, but not because she wasn't into what he was doing.

She didn't want to lose herself to him.

And she was already well on her way to doing just that from his kisses and touches alone.

Bill's hand had found its way to her cheek, and he tilted her head up to look at him. He gazed down at her with that soft smile that put the crinkles at the corners of his eyes and made her belly melt and her knees wobble.

Ray kept as straight a face as she could as she turned

away from him, leaning her face up and into the spray, cleaning herself up quickly before stepping out without another word.

Suddenly, it was loud in the bathroom. She exited quickly, toweling off and finding clean clothes to wear. While she pulled her pants on, which was hard to do when her legs were still damp, she could hear the shower so clearly.

Just as clear as the thought that had dawned on her.

She wasn't over him. Not a bit.

Her heart still thought of Bill *as her fated mate.*

"Esme got back to me," he said, finally turning off the shower and stepping out.

Ray paused, then quickly went back to getting her bra on.

Another difficult task when her body was damp. "What did she say?"

Bill paused again, and Ray couldn't bear to look back at him.

"Basically? That I'm a fucking idiot," he said. "But you knew that already."

Ray's breath hitched.

Yeah, she did know it, and she wasn't in the mood to have this conversation right now. Not with him, and not after what they'd just done, which was why she finished dressing, grabbed her bag, slid into her shoes, and walked out of there before she started thinking too hard about the weird little thoughts and feelings that were suddenly creeping in.

CHAPTER
NINE

Bill already knew Ray would avoid him for the rest of the day. He wasn't an idiot.

But he couldn't stand the thought of her going out and being hit on by other singles on the cruise.

Some stupid human with too much ego was the last thing Bill wanted to deal with.

Which forced him into the uncomfortable position of following around his own mate, from a distance of course, and making sure nothing out of bounds happened with one of the other passengers on the ship.

He felt like such a fucking creep. He hated it, but it didn't take long before his mind was put at ease as he watched Ray meet up with another woman.

A tall, tanned woman, probably Italian, who definitely gave off another shifter vibe.

Bear, he thought.

The two women greeted each other like old friends and immediately walked into the nearest bar.

Bill watched them order drinks before he decided enough was enough, and he walked away.

Bill needed to back off.

Much as it pained him to think about, there was only one real test to this, and he had to wait before it could be done.

So, he went back to the gym, forced himself to relax, and even managed to mingle with some of the other passengers before he grabbed his dinner and returned to the room he and Ray were sharing.

He glared at the pillows and blankets that were still in the chair in the corner.

He couldn't believe Ray thought he would be sleeping on the floor.

Well, that didn't happen last night, and it wasn't happening now.

It was a little on the early side when he stripped entirely naked and crawled under the covers of the crisp, fresh sheets.

He loved fresh bedsheets.

Bill was still getting used to being around so many people, to being in a situation where he wasn't always on the lookout for someone carrying weapons or getting ready to eliminate him. He still had no idea how he ended up in the situation at all—why had Esme Baer started a conversation with him in the first place? Why did she want him on the ship?

When she'd invited him, she'd told him that she could just tell things about people, and what she knew from looking at Bill was that he needed a vacation. A time to unwind.

And a chance for his heart to feel happy again.

In any ordinary situation, Bill would have blown off the stranger, but her invitation felt more like the command of an alpha, something he couldn't refuse, and so he'd agreed.

He'd yet to decide if he was happy he'd done so or not.

Vaguely, Bill listened to the sounds of the cruise ship, felt the motion from the ocean itself, and closed his eyes to force himself to not take in so much information all at once.

It was too dangerous. Easy to get lost in the information. To zone out while trying to pinpoint every little thing.

Which was when things got the most dangerous. When he couldn't focus on one thing because he was focusing on *everything*.

He must have dozed off a little because it felt like suddenly more time had passed, and he snapped back into full awareness when he heard the keycard and the following click of the locks on his door.

It opened. Light from the outside briefly spilled into his room, and Ray's sweet scent entered with it.

Bill relaxed, keeping his eyes closed, listening to her padding into the room.

She stood at the end of the bed. He could tell she watched him.

Frustrated that he was back in bed instead of on the floor?

Well, that was too bad.

Still, his mind raced. The wild animal of his inner Grizzly easily taking over the calmer, more focused senses that came from the cybernetic implants in his head.

Come on. You can do it. I know you want to.

Then, a sigh. He heard the gentle rustle of fabric, and —*sweet relief*—she was getting undressed and getting into bed with him.

He briefly felt cooler air along his side and his legs as she lifted the blanket and slid inside.

He opened his eyes, slowly and calmly, then looked at her.

Shifter vision was pretty good in the dark, but with his implants from his former boss, he could see Ray as clearly as though the morning sun was coming in through the windows.

Not as pretty as the real thing. This artificial vision wouldn't hold a candle to golden sunlight caressing her shoulders.

"Sorry," she said softly, whispering as though someone might hear them. "Did I wake you?"

"No," he said. It was partly true.

He cast his eyes down, getting a proper look at her, and he could already tell she wasn't wearing a damn thing. She'd taken off all of her clothes, the same as he had.

He reached his hand out, stopping, hesitating before touching her cheek.

He shouldn't have bothered. She met him halfway again, pushing herself into his arms, climbing into his lap, and kissing him.

Yes. Fuck, yes.

He fucking knew it. This was the test, and she was in his arms, not smelling of anything other than the perfumes used in the spas and the food she'd eaten, and maybe a little of the alcohol from those weak little drinks she'd been enjoying without him.

She didn't smell like other males, and her eyes were still clear, the motions of her hands on his shoulders and around his neck sure and strong.

"You got a condom?"

Oh, right.

Bill had to laugh at himself for nearly forgetting again, but grabbing one from his bag didn't spoil the mood, and his little red panda was back in his arms in no time at all.

She rode him at a pace that wasn't too slow and not too

fast either. It wasn't gentle but definitely not harsh or rough.

It was fucking perfect, was what it was.

They made love for what felt like hours, and even when they weren't having sex, it was a lot of kissing, stroking, and just holding.

Very little talking.

That was the worrisome part.

"Ray, you and I should—"

"Later," she insisted. "Can we just... talk about it later? I'm tired, and I just want to have this for tonight. I want to sleep."

Fuck. How the hell was he supposed to say no to that?

She did look tired and a little unsure when the act was done, and she was settling into her pillows, but he knew what this really was.

She was avoiding him.

They were silent for a while. Long enough that he thought she fell asleep before Ray finally asked.

"Bill? Why did you leave?"

Fuck. Bill pretended to not hear her. He pretended to sleep.

He needed to do this, but he just couldn't find a way to. The story was too convoluted.

Lilly, too dangerous.

The implants. The males she'd kidnapped and locked away.

He'd witnessed it all and had no way to escape and had been terrified that crazy vampire bitch would do something to Ray.

"Bill?" Ray whispered. "Are you sleeping?"

Again, he stayed quiet, letting her believe it as she snuggled up with him.

At least they had that.

He was failing at his mission, and he could imagine Esme kicking their door in right then, telling him he better just come out with it.

The thought alone was *almost* enough to make him speak, but he didn't. He hated talking about anything, never mind *that*. He was shit at getting the right words out, but that never mattered to Ray before.

Bill just wanted to give her what she wanted.

He curled his arm around her shoulders, pretending to be doing that while he slept.

She didn't seem to mind.

Ray was next to him, and things were... relatively pleasant. He figured that was the most he could ask for at the moment, and he didn't want to fuck that up.

The next morning he woke up to the bed empty, which was already weird enough since he was normally the one to wake up first, but it seemed all he'd been doing since getting on this damn boat was sleeping.

Maybe it was messing with the wires in his head.

Or his inner Grizzly wanted to hibernate every time he was near his mate.

Either way, he showered and dressed, deciding to join the rest of the ship.

They were docking at the private islands today, it seemed, and thank God for that.

There were two islands. One was meant for the shifters and their current mates or travel buddies—anyone who already knew about the shifter secret—to be on. A place where shifters could go and let out their inner animals for a time.

Apparently, too many shifters on a ship, cluttered together and unable to let their animals out because of the humans on board, was enough to make some people antsy, regardless of how fancy the place was.

The other island was for the humans who were unaware of shifters. Both islands would have places for shopping, photographs, and general sightseeing, but the island for shifters had been marked on his ticket when Esme set him up with this ride.

Apparently, a few years back, they had marked the tickets with the letters VIP to indicate a shifter allowed on the secret island. But then, one too many rich humans complained about not being able to get onto the VIP list and were angry about what they were possibly missing out on, on the other island.

Nowadays, the second island was simply marketed as to not overwhelm the villages with too many tourists at once who could not be kept track of.

It seemed to work.

After the last couple of nights, Bill was looking forward to letting out his inner bear and maybe doing some hunting.

Ever since the implants, what had been... done to him, well, it had been easier to hold back on his wilder side.

Even when he'd been with Ray, much as he'd loved her, he'd felt a cold, distant reservation within him that was only silenced during their most passionate moments.

And since he'd walked away from her, to hide from Lilly the thing he cared about most, that cloudiness, that lack of connection he felt to anything just seemed to get worse.

Not so much now.

Ever since he walked into their room for the first time and saw Ray standing there, it was like his implants had short-circuited, allowing him to feel like his old self again.

And making him feel the need to let the bear out.

His wild side wanted to roar.

Fuck. He needed off this boat, was what he needed.

He lined up for the tinder going to shifter island, smelling the other shifters around him, as well as something a little familiar.

It raised the hairs on the back of his neck. He searched around, eyes focusing, scanning, but the faces were all strangers to him. He might have walked by these people on the boat a few times already, but they had all blended in with the crowd, and he couldn't pick out anyone as familiar.

Was it Ray? Or that friend of hers?

Hard to say, but Bill decided to let it go, the smell went away when he got onto one of the shuttle boats, and they sped toward the island.

It was beautiful there.

The islands around here were paradises set aside almost explicitly for the tourists.

There was indeed some shopping and sightseeing to be had on the shifter island, but the people who lived and worked here were all either shifters themselves, or came from families who knew of them, so if anyone wandered onto the beaches and caught sight of a woman shifting into a honey badger or something, it wouldn't matter.

The villages on these islands apparently made their money through tourism, flying people on and off the islands, selling whatever art or trinkets they made themselves, and fishing.

The fishing part excited Bill the most.

He was dying for a thick cut of salmon.

The trinkets pulled his attention at a close second.

What better way to beg and grovel into Ray's forgiveness than a necklace from a paradise island?

He knew she would be coming to the island today. Almost all the shifters were, and he could tell she was getting antsy to let out her little red panda.

God, he missed her already, couldn't wait to see her and pull his little red panda bear into his arms like a tiny, cuddly teddy bear.

As a joke, she'd once given him an actual teddy bear, then laughed when he'd made a face at it.

"You said you like teddy bears," she'd laughed.

"Not really," he'd growled, staring at the bear like it had just insulted his mother. "This isn't remotely the same as holding onto you," he'd said.

Ray had blushed then, as though still unsure about taking compliments, even from him, and grumbled something about it being a gift and how he needed to accept it.

He never cuddled with that bear, because it wasn't Ray and not what he'd been looking for.

But he still had the damn thing.

It was one of the things he made sure to take from her apartment when he'd packed up his shit and left her behind.

He found the shops. Little stalls that looked more like a craft market than anything, but mixed in were clothes, food, and the trinkets he was searching for.

There were rough-looking rings, necklaces, and earrings all made out of seashells, paintings, a few friendship bracelets, and anything with hand-painted pictures.

It all looked really nice, if he was honest.

In the end, he hoped to find something with a bear on it, but when on a cruise ship vacation and visiting a tropical island, he wasn't shocked when he didn't find anything with either Grizzly bears or red pandas on them. These islands weren't exactly home to native ursine, or the non-similar red panda family.

He settled for a necklace made of small shells with a smooth, oval stone focal point painted with a red-haired mermaid.

Ray loved that movie. For a woman who was afraid of any body of water deeper than a bathtub, she loved mermaid movies, Finding Nemo, anything to do with the ocean.

And if there had been some sort of deep-sea documentary that showed off the ocean in bright colors and peaceful schools of fish, well, God help Bill if he ever tried getting his hands on the remote and searching for something else to watch on Netflix or whatever.

Satisfied with his purchase, he paid the vendor and was given a small white box to hold the necklace in and a teal-colored ribbon to tie it off with.

Bill left there feeling proud of himself, the bright sun overhead, the warmth and smell of saltwater in the air making him feel pretty good about this whole thing for the first time in a long time.

Esme wouldn't have done this if she didn't think he had a chance, and he was going to make it right with Ray.

They were going to enjoy the rest of their cruise vacation. He would let Ray know what happened with his old boss, tell her that things were all right now, that it had been long enough that he was sure Lilly wasn't coming after him, and then they'd go home together.

On his way back to the beach, he started searching for Ray.

It was possible she wouldn't get on the shuttle boat to come over to the island with her fear of the water.

But she was still a shifter. A cute, cuddly little red

panda, but even she would need to let her animal out to roam, and she wouldn't be able to do that on the ship.

Bill moved back to the beach. There were so many people there. A few wolves, big cats, a damn dragon, of all things. Those were rare.

He got a feeling in the back of his neck. The feeling he didn't like that usually meant someone was...

Watching him.

He looked around. Old instincts rose back to the surface, as well as the paranoid fear that maybe Lilly hadn't decided to let him go after all.

No. She was a vampire and wouldn't be caught dead on a beach, and the implants she gave him, while expensive, weren't so all-consuming that she would need her investment returned.

Still, he rubbed the back of his neck, moving away from the beach.

Ray wasn't there anyway.

Bill sought out the space to store his purchase and clothes, then shift, but that feeling followed him.

The longer it did, the more irritated he became.

Bill reasoned that the most likely scenario was that he was being watched by one of the other men from the ship who had an interest in Ray.

Right. That was probably it.

Some idiot alpha with a jealousy complex was pissed off that the sexy redhead wasn't reciprocating his advances and coming back to Bill again and again and maybe wanted to pick a bone with him.

If they tried it, Bill would be breaking bones, not picking them.

He stopped heading to the storage lockers. Now he was searching for a spot to have that confrontation, tucking the small box with Ray's mermaid necklace into his pocket before turning around with a heavy sigh.

"What are you doing following me?"

He glanced around. The ocean behind him, the tropical trees, and plant life created a barrier that gave some semblance of privacy.

With all that in the way, even his improved vision couldn't pick out where the guy was.

Which meant his pursuer was very good at stealth.

"You've got some training, but I know you're there. Get out here, now."

Bill picked up on the sounds of harsh cursing. Some of those long-leafed plants rustled and moved out of the way, and a face Bill never thought he would see again emerged.

The man looked like your average tourist ready to kick back and enjoy the sun and sand. His modified body wore shorts, a Hawaiian shirt, and flips flops, of all things.

Except, the quiet anger on his face looked less like it belonged to someone enjoying a vacation and more like that of a man who knew he was about to commit a murder.

Holy fuck.

"Dallas?"

"Yeah." Dallas brought his hands up, his mechanical arm crackling the knuckles of his biological one. "It's me."

CHAPTER

TEN

R AY SUFFERED THROUGH THE SHUTTLE BOAT, HER TEETH CLENCHED up tight, her body stiffer than some of those surfboards she saw out on the water, until the boat slowed down and pulled up to a dock.

She left the boat gratefully, and if she wasn't worried about taking in a mouthful of sand, she might have kissed the ground.

No. The first thing she did was find the nearest bathroom and hide in it, catching her breath, telling herself that all was all right, and talking her stomach out of throwing up the breakfast she'd had that morning.

Her stomach bulged a little. The crêpes, fruits, and yogurt, along with bacon, eggs, and sausages, had been too much to resist.

She knew eating so much would give her a sore belly, but she'd decided to roll those dice.

Before a trip on a smaller boat? Not the smartest choice of her life.

After sitting in her stall long enough, making sure her stomach was settled and nothing was about to come up,

Ray checked her makeup in the mirror, took a breath, and left the ladies' room.

She joined the rest of the people on the beach, watching the gentle ocean waves wash up onto the sand.

Back and forth while shifters chased their mates around.

Larger shifters went after smaller ones, who pretended they couldn't run faster, letting themselves be caught up in the water.

Humans laughing, shifters chirping, chittering, and barking. All playing. Enjoying their day.

A few humans stayed on the beach, towels and umbrellas out and at the ready. The shifters who changed into animals with thick fur coats found refuge in the shade of those umbrellas, or even the trees. The big cats did what cats always did, and splayed themselves out in the sun.

It was such a beautiful scene. Ray found herself beyond grateful that she'd brought her work bag to the island.

Changing into animal shape suddenly wasn't the most prominent thing on her mind as she found a spot where no one might accidentally kick up any sand at her while chasing after their mate.

She ended up in a spot under the trees, looking over the water. About ten feet away from her, two ladies had set up their towels and were huddled together, smearing sunscreen over their tanned shoulders and toned bellies.

It took Ray a hot minute before she realized the scents the women were giving off were ones of soft pleasure. Not the kind that came from sex, but the pleasure of just having one's hands on their mate and enjoying the moment.

She suddenly felt hot under the collar. She'd chosen this spot because she hadn't wanted to interrupt any couples. Still, it didn't seem as though she was in the way right now, and getting up would draw more attention, so for the moment, Ray stayed where she was, pulling out her pencils.

Working freelance was awesome. Her job could be tedious at times, especially when it came to digitizing her work. Mostly no one was overly impressed when any of the patterns she'd made ended up on a packet of napkins that were sold in a Walmart. Still, she liked it, and being on the beach, she felt a moment of pleasant inspiration as she focused on the leaf of a plant she couldn't name and started sketching it out with her watercolor pencils.

Bill had been the exception. He was the one person who had always seemed impressed. He'd always looked at what she did as though she wasn't just making doodles and getting ridiculously lucky earning a living by selling them.

She smiled as she remembered the time she told him her patterns were getting printed on some towels and sold in a big department store.

He'd been over the moon for her, and they'd gone out to dinner and a movie to celebrate before coming home to passionate kisses and tripping their way to her bed.

They hadn't made it to her room, but the couch had worked out just fine.

Ray stopped coloring the leaves she'd been drawing, staring at the page without seeing them.

She glanced over at the nearby couple. They weren't doing anything, just laying back on their towels, close enough that their shoulders touched.

Ray glanced back out at the water. She spotted a few couples kissing softly. Nothing too involved. No one was sticking their tongues in each other's throats, but it was just more of that easy pleasure.

A mated love.

Her stomach clenched, pain and jealousy hitting her hard as she thought about how she'd had that once.

She and Bill had been like that.

She'd thought he was the one.

And then he just left. All of his stuff out of her apartment one day and a text message telling her he was sorry, but it was over.

Now he was back, and she'd slept with him—not just the fucking, but the actual peaceful cuddly sleeping—stupidly thinking... she was actually considering...

Ray swallowed hard over the lump in her throat, rubbing at the back of her neck.

Without knowing why, her eye was drawn to the far side of the beach, and she froze at the sight of Bill.

He was scanning the beach in that strange, mechanical way that he did.

Looking for her?

He seemed to look her way for just a second. Ray opened her mouth to call out to him, but then he turned quickly and marched off, his hands clenched and shoulders tight.

Ray's heart suddenly slammed like it was trying to break through her skin.

She didn't have the chance to contemplate whether he'd seen her and marched away when she spotted someone following him.

She noted the way the stranger stared at the back of Bill's head, his eyes glowing red... this was a problem.

Ray scrambled to pack away her supplies, not bothering with keeping everything nice, neat, and clean like she usually preferred, since there might be a problem on the way.

Why would anyone want to fight Bill? Sometimes

alphas got hot-headed. Bill might have pissed someone off at the poker table or in the gym, and if that guy was going to try picking a fight, or sucking punching him, then Ray didn't care what their history was. She was not about to let that happen.

She rushed down the sandy beach, hating how it made it difficult for her to properly run, but when that man was briefly out of sight, she panicked again, until she spotted him, there in the distance, following Bill down a narrow, dirt path through the trees and plants.

What the hell? How could Bill not notice someone was right behind him?

He was usually better about these things, but Ray didn't care about any of that as she raced after them.

Red pandas were definitely not made to be rushing through terrain like this. It was one whole struggle as she fought her way over the lumpy path.

Just because people walked along it enough to stop any growth didn't mean it was smooth.

She finally made it to them, wheezing a little for breath just as the man with the mechanical arm marched towards Bill, his hands clenched into tight fists.

Bill saw him coming. Ray was aware of that much, but something happened. She worked on autopilot, using the whole weight of her supply bag she'd been lugging around the ship this entire time, swinging it hard at the back of the stranger's head.

Bill saw her first. His eyes flew wide, that eery blue glow brighter than ever.

The assailant's mechanical arm shot up, grabbing the bag before it could make contact with his head.

"What the—"

With unnatural speed, the man tossed her bag to the

side and then caught her by the throat, his metal fingers holding firmly with the promise of how easily they could crush her windpipe.

"Hey!" Bill roared, but he didn't have to do anything at all because the second the man looked at her, his face contorted.

It was as if he saw the thing of his nightmares as his hand immediately fell away, and he stepped back in horror. "Rita?"

"What? No!" Ray yelled, angry and scared and rubbing her throat.

Bill punched the cyborg in the side of the head, using his momentary distraction against him.

Ray shrieked a little and flew out of the way as the two men tumbled to the rock and sand.

The beach here wasn't nearly as clean and soft as the location meant for sunbathing, but it didn't matter to the two men. Especially when Bill suddenly shifted, shredding his clothes and turning into his enormous Grizzly bear.

His eyes were round and black with rage. His mouth sent slobber flying as he roared and lunged at his foe, trying to get those massive teeth around the cyborg's head.

A few things fell into slow motion for her.

Namely, the look in his eyes. They were completely dark at first glance, but peering more closely, she saw that blue glow. The one that appeared when he was worked up about something.

It sometimes happened when he was having a great workout in the gym. Also happened when they got into an argument.

And, of course, she'd seen it in bed.

But now, with his oversized bear eyes, she saw more than just the blue glow.

There were moving parts behind his eyes. Something unnatural there that caught her attention in an iron grip, and refused to let go.

Those moving parts were new, and they weren't natural.

He'd had work done on him.

Maybe not as much as the guy with the metallic arm who grabbed onto Bill's bear jaws, holding off the bite of death.

The man Bill was fighting was a *cyborg*.

Was Bill, too?

Clarity hit her, then. She'd thought Bill had left her because of something *she'd* done wrong, but now it was so obvious. Bill had left because something had happened to him. A secret that was too big to share with her.

"Dallas!"

A scream sounded behind Ray, waking her up and taking her attention off the deathmatch and her realization about her mate—because *yes,* Bill *was* her true fated mate.

Ray whirled around, coming face to face with... a mirror image of herself.

The other woman stared at the cyborg and bear rolling around in the sand, her eyes wide, terror and shock clearly hitting her hard enough that she didn't notice Ray standing right there.

Until a moment later, when she did cast a glance her way.

When she did, the terror immediately melted from her face, exchanged for something closer to disbelief and shock.

Ray blinked a couple of times, and the vision of the woman in front of her didn't vanish.

It wasn't an exact copy.

Of course their clothes were different. This woman

wore a stylish yellow romper, compared to Ray's pale green understated sundress.

The woman's long red hair was also much darker. Almost a chestnut, with several greys streaking through it. Her eyes were dark as well.

Nothing at all like Ray's red hair and pale brown eyes.

Didn't matter. Just from looking at her, it was apparent that this was one of Ray's sisters, whom Ray had dared to hope might actually be on this vacation with her.

"Rita? Hey! What's going—"

Another woman rushed through the shrubs and over the uneven path, stopping sharply at the sight of the fighting. She looked at Rita, and her eyes popped comically wide at the sight of Ray.

Another doppelgänger. Another sister. This one blond, wearing a pale blue bandeau maxi dress.

Both sisters standing right there, staring at Ray.

She felt a little dumb and frozen. Bill was behind her trying to kill a man, and she could only stand there smiling stupidly.

A man came in behind the second woman, reaching out and grabbing her hand. "Baby, what did you—"

He had one green eye and one mechanical eye. One of his arms was mechanical like the male Bill fought with, but the shorts he wore showed that both of his legs were mechanical as well.

"Holy shit," he said, rushing in to help his friend.

Because of course he was going to help his friend.

Ray snapped out of it, feeling like a massive jerk for just standing there, regardless of who was in front of her, and she did something incredibly stupid.

She jumped into the fight, trying to pull off the man

with the mechanical legs when he attempted to body-check Bill away.

"Stop! Stop, it's a mistake! Please!"

She had no idea if it was a mistake, but these were her sisters. They were right here. These men could only be their mates, and this had to be a misunderstanding.

It had to be.

The male reached back to grab at her and shove her away, much like his friend had done, but the second he got a decent look at her, he stopped.

Confusion and worry in his eyes, but he wasn't hurting her, and she had his attention.

"You have to stop!" Ray begged. "It's a mistake! Stop them!"

She sure as hell couldn't, and not for the first time she wished she was a larger animal, something that could help in a fight, instead of relying on others to help.

She didn't even know if she could rely on this guy.

"Dallas! Stop it!" the first woman shouted.

Ray needed to get Bill's attention.

Dallas managed to get out from under the bear, and Ray didn't care what they were fighting about. She just needed them to quit it.

She stepped between the oversized Grizzly and the cyborg with the metal arm, her hand held out, hoping desperately that he wasn't so far gone that he wouldn't recognize her.

Bill stopped short, and Ray never thought she would see a face so expressive on a bear before.

"Stop," she said.

Dallas didn't seem to get the hint anymore. "You dirty motherfucker!"

Ray whipped around.

Her sisters, and the man with the metal legs, were now standing in front of Dallas, trying to hold him back the same way Ray was blocking the bear from attacking.

"You're with her? You fucking did *this*!"

Ray didn't know what he meant. She didn't get it, but she knew it had to be a mistake. "Listen, I'm sorry for whatever you think happened, but you've got the wrong guy."

Dallas looked at her, his expression twisting again, as if he didn't know what to make of the woman in front of him. Then he shook his head. "What... what is this? Are you *with* him?"

"I am," Ray didn't even have to think about it. "Who are you?"

"Ray," Bill said. She looked back, seeing he was in his human shape, completely naked and with the markings of a bruise forming on his shoulders where Dallas had grabbed him. "I need to talk to you."

"Did he tell you who he is?" Dallas snapped. "What he did?"

This was all getting to be too fucking much. She couldn't take it. "Whatever he did, that's for me and him to work out, all right?"

"No, Ray," Bill said, his touch gentle when he took her by the arm.

There was something in his voice that made her snap her attention right to him. She stared at him long and hard, a strange panic welling up within her.

Bill looked at the two men and women, his gaze hard and suspicious, before looking back down at her. "We need to talk."

Her throat was suddenly dry. Ray didn't want to talk, but she got the feeling this wasn't something she was going to get out of. "Is this why you left?"

He nodded. "Yeah."

Ray's knees shook. She grabbed onto Bill's forearm, holding her balance and trying to keep her head on steady.

Whatever was going on between the men had to come second to the fact that her sisters were there.

The sisters she'd been looking for, ever since she'd learned they existed.

She was suddenly feeling a little queasy again.

"I think we should all sit down and figure out what's going on here," the first woman—Rita, Ray surmised—spoke up, seeming to be the only calm head in the group while she smiled softly at Ray. "Nice to meet you, sis,"

CHAPTER

ELEVEN

He'd thought he smelled something familiar, but in his wildest imagination, he wouldn't have guessed it was Dallas.

Fucking Dallas was here.

He hadn't seen him on the ship, but there were so many people on that damn boat that it only made sense he wouldn't see every single person.

Even with his vision implants.

He wouldn't have been able to smell him in a crowd, either. Too many people, too many mingling scents and perfumes, sweat, salty air.

There was no way he would have noticed Dallas before now.

The two other women who were picture-perfect copies of Ray, with the exception of the hair and eye color?

Well, unless he saw their faces, he wouldn't have noticed them either. One of these ladies could have been walking ahead of him at any time, and he wouldn't have known they were related to Ray if he hadn't seen their faces.

He knew she had relatives she didn't know. She'd told him before. Two sisters. A couple of Racoon shifters. All separated at birth.

They were here. Dallas was here, as was this other cyborg guy who clearly had work done on him, likely from Lilly, Bill's old vampire boss.

And Esme knew all of it.

It would be so much easier if Esme just spelled everything out for them.

Where's the fun in that? Bill could imagine her saying.

But it was just her way of doing things. If you tell people everything, they can look at it, analyze it, rip it to pieces before they ever even give it a shot.

And besides, looking out at all the people there, it looked like Esme had a *lot* of clients. Anyone was lucky to have her lend a hand in leading them to their mates. There was no way she could hold that hand through everything. That's why she made them work things out for themselves.

Bill sat cross-legged on the sand, the other two ladies—Rita and Roquette—and their mates—Dallas and Aaron—across from him. The only good thing about the situation was that Ray was right beside him.

Not just beside him while they had this little therapy session, but she was practically in his lap, leaning against him, her hand protectively on his thigh as she stared down the two males who'd picked a fight with him.

Defending him when he didn't deserve it. When she didn't know why she had to defend him at all.

He fucking loved her.

"So, these two men used to work with you?" Ray asked, looking from the two males, to her sisters, and then to Bill.

Bill clenched his jaw. "Dallas and I briefly worked together. I've ever seen Aaron here in passing."

The man had been hired on later. Bill had only seen him once before, so he hadn't recognized him in the frenzy of the fight he and Dallas had been in the middle of.

"And your boss, Lilly, she wanted to do all this work on you guys?" Ray gently touched his face before yanking her hand back, as though burned. "That's why your eyes turn blue?"

"Yeah."

On the other hand, Dallas' eyes were a bright shade of red.

Yeah, he was definitely pissed off.

"This asshole kept me in a fucking coffin," Dallas spat. "He saw what that bitch was doing to me, and he just looked the other way."

It was *not* that simple. Bill would say that to his dying day, but how was he supposed to square that circle to the guy he'd wronged while sitting across from him?

Ray didn't seem to have any trouble with that, however. She didn't have the same sense of guilt that Bill did. "There's no way he would have done anything to you unless he had to."

"Lady, you can keep your mouth shut and stay out of this because it has nothing to do with you," Dallas snapped.

"Watch it," Bill growled. "You grabbed her by the throat. You don't get to talk to her like that."

"Bill," Ray said.

"Right, because that would be going too far, wouldn't it?" Dallas interjected, clearly mocking Bill, his face twisted and hateful.

The thing that pulled Dallas back, what made his

expression soften, was the hand of his mate, Rita, gently touching his arm.

Pulling him back from the brink.

Bill looked at Rita, and then he looked at Dallas. "You'd do anything to keep her safe. Don't try to pretend you wouldn't. If you had your woman to protect while Lilly made you work, then you would absolutely keep your head down and do as you were told."

"Fuck. You." Dallas punctuated each word, his shoulders bunching again.

"Dallas," Rita said, her arm coming around his shoulders, trying desperately to keep the calm. "I know this is all so strange, but maybe we should hear him out?"

"You just want to—" Dallas cut himself off, snapping his lips shut, as though desperate to keep himself from saying something he was going to regret.

Bill didn't blame him. "Esme clearly brought us all here on purpose. The four of you came for some romantic getaway, and I showed up to—"

"He came with me to help me find my sisters," Ray said quickly. "And to... rekindle our relationship."

"Rekindle?" Rita asked, looking between them.

Ray cleared her throat. "Yeah, uh, the stress of his job and me looking for the two of you didn't exactly leave any room for romance, you know?"

Bill didn't understand. She could definitely throw him under the bus. Let loose what a terrible person he was for bailing on her when things got too heated with Lilly.

Instead, she defended him. Told a lie to the two males who hated him the most, and her own sisters she wished to have a relationship with.

All to prevent him from looking like the exact son of a bitch he actually was.

"I didn't want Lilly hurting Ray." He put his arm around her shoulders, holding her close. "Lilly didn't know I had someone."

They needed to know why he did what he did. Why he stood there and let atrocious things happen in front of his own cybernetically-enhanced eyes.

It wouldn't take anything back, but maybe it would help them understand.

Maybe not hate him so much.

And allow Ray the chance she'd always wanted to be with her family.

"I was never sure of the exact details, but I knew Lilly had some sort of interest in you," that part he said to Dallas. "So when she kept you on ice, I didn't do anything to help. I didn't unplug you because I didn't want her turning on me and coming after Ray."

Dallas shook his head, looking away from him, still clearly furious.

"I guess that makes sense," he muttered.

"How did you get away?" Ray asked the question to Dallas.

Rita smiled, sitting up a little straighter, and answered for him. "I busted him out."

"You... did?" Bill didn't know what to say to that. His first instinct was to not believe her at all. Really? She'd managed to sneak onto Lilly's property and take what Lilly wanted the most?

It had to be true, though. Dallas looked at Rita with such pride, his mouth pulled into the kind of smile a man only got when he was staring at his sweetheart.

"I did," Rita replied. "I would have never *known* to, though, if Esme Baer hadn't sent me there."

A murmur at the name *Esme Baer* went around the

group, telling Bill that the matchmaker had also played a part in Aaron and Roquette's relationship.

Aaron kept looking at Dallas with that simmering distrust in his green and mechanical eyes. The difference was that he was more curious and reserved than the boiling, bubbling anger Dallas seemed to have for him.

Bill didn't like that. He looked pointedly at Aaron's legs. "So, what was your excuse for getting the implants? Must be some top-of-the-line shit."

"It was either the implants, or I stayed in a wheelchair for the rest of my life," Aaron said. "I got out as soon as I could, too. I didn't like what Lilly wanted me to do."

Ah, so that explained why this guy wasn't quite so ready to rip his head off.

"When did you two meet?" Ray asked her sisters, clearly eager to get off the topic of evil vampires.

Bill had no idea how she was taking all of this so well. She was a damn saint.

"At the Baer's Christmas party this past year," Rita said, glancing at the other woman. "I mean, I hadn't looked into it much before. Raccoon shifters don't always stay in the family, so boy was I surprised when we met there. At first, I thought we could be cousins, but the DNA test showed that we were closer than that."

"Sisters." Ray nodded.

Dallas and Bill exchanged a glare. Their mates were related. That was a disaster for two men who wanted to strangle each other.

"I don't expect you to be good with me, ever," Bill said. "But we could be civil for our mates."

Dallas' neck tightened. "Civil. For now."

"Did you know about me?" Ray asked, ignoring Bill and Dallas and going right for the meat of the thing.

Bill didn't blame her. She'd wanted to meet her sisters for years. Had known about them before Bill had even met her. She would have a one-track mind for a long while, wanting to learn all she could about her sisters. His beef with Dallas could wait.

"Not exactly," Rita said. "But with the help of Harmony, I learned that I did have family out there when I'd once thought I was completely alone."

"So, Harmony and Esme sent us all here as a type of family reunion," Roquette mused.

Aaron made a distasteful face. "I don't like thinking of a matchmaking cruise as a family reunion."

"It is, though, in a way," Roquette teased, nudging him a little.

"Do you two know our aunt?" Ray asked.

Both women's eyes widened. "Aunt?" Rita asked.

At the same time, Roquette asked, "We have an aunt?"

Ray deflated a little and nodded. "Yeah. She's a full raccoon shifter. Like both of you, right?"

The two women confirmed it.

"But you're not?" Rita asked, leaning forward to sniff the air.

"I'm a red panda," Ray offered. Bill knew it was a rare shifter type, and not many people could identify it.

"Oh, wow."

Both Rita and Roquette looked surprised.

"And I thought I was odd," Roquette murmured. At Ray's curious head-tilt, Roquette smiled bashfully. "I'm a white raccoon. So, I smell like a raccoon, but when folks see me for the first time, they're often thrown a little."

"That's cool!" Ray smiled brightly.

"So, you know about an aunt?" Rita asked. "What else do you know about our family? Esme connected Roquette and me, but she only knew we were related because she'd met us and, you know, two girls who looked the same and were both raccoon shifters. We were disappointed that she didn't have the answers to *why* we'd been... well, why we grew up separated."

"My adoptive parents knew very little, and they only told me any of it when I was an adult." Ray took a deep breath. "From what I understand, it had something to do with the different types of shifters we were. One of our parents was from a red panda family, and the other was raccoon. Our mother was most like a red panda, but..."

"But what?" Roquette asked.

Rita placed a hand on Roquette's, answering for Ray. "Raccoons aren't exactly looked well on. You know, being trash pandas isn't as fancy as red pandas."

"We're technically not pandas," Ray said. "But they're not raccoons either."

"So we're talking about a red panda woman..." Rita trailed off, but Bill could see the realization dawning in both the raccoon women.

Ray picked it back up. "I believe our mother was forced to give us up, and to give up our father. There's no record of them, anywhere, but I was able to find an aunt. Our father's sister."

"But you haven't visited her yet?" Roquette asked.

"I haven't tracked her down. I only know that she exists."

Bill squeezed her shoulder. "Well, now that you've found your sisters, maybe it's time to track down the aunt."

Ray looked up at him sharply, her soft brown eyes softening as she nodded and melted against him.

"I still don't like you," Dallas said. "But I'll tolerate you for Rita. You want to find your aunt? That's fine. I'm on board, but Bill? You can stay the hell away from me at all times. The ladies can mingle without you and me getting in each other's faces."

Bill nodded. "Understood."

"Good." Dallas shot to his feet, glaring down at Bill, and then looking a little more unsure at Rita.

Rita smiled up at him, stroking his leg. "I can go with you."

Dallas took a breath. "No, stay here. Catch up with your sisters. I need a drink. I'll be... back on the beach."

He clearly didn't want to leave his mate with the man he hated most in the world, regardless of there being another male he trusted, and two other females.

Some instincts even robotic implants could not override.

"I want a drink, too," Ray said, shocking Bill by getting to her feet, pulling him up with her. "I want to keep talking to you both. I do. I just need to talk to Bill for a few minutes. Can we come back with drinks?"

Ray seemed so hopeful, so terrified the two ladies and their mates would show no interest, would consider the meeting over, and want to go back to their lives without her.

Bill didn't know what he would be able to do for her if that happened.

How would he be able to mend a heart crushed like that?

Rita and Roquette looked at each other, then at her.

"We're fine with that," Rita said.

"Yeah," Roquette added.

Ray heaved a sigh, her smile brighter than the beach sun above them. "Perfect. Uh, you guys stay here. Bill and I'll be right back."

"Any drinks you get for us, make sure they're in sealed containers or bottles," Dallas called after them.

It also sounded like Rita smacked him hard in the arm for saying it, but he didn't take it back.

And Bill didn't stop as Ray dragged him away, down the lumpy path, away from her sisters she'd been dying to meet for years.

All so she could talk with him.

So he could finally tell her the truth.

TWELVE

RAY HAULED HER BAG A LITTLE TIGHTER OVER HER SHOULDER. SHE felt Bill following after her as she marched ahead, which was a damn good thing because she definitely had a bone to pick with him, and she needed to do that away from the two people Ray had wanted to impress most in the world.

"Ray."

"Not yet."

She needed someplace away from the beach. Away from Rita and Roquette and their mates. Away from everything so she could ask what she needed to ask in private.

Fortunately, there was another place. Somewhere that seemed quiet enough with no signs of any couples who snuck away to make out or have sex.

"Ray."

Ray whirled on him. "Was that why you left? Seriously?"

He looked her right in the eyes, his expression as stony and hard to read as ever.

"Yes."

Ray struggled against the urge to yank her hair out. "You... you told me you worked in security or something."

"I did."

"With a crazy vampire lady who was into doing that to people?"

She thought of Aaron and his legs. She didn't care that he'd chosen it to stay out of a wheelchair. What she cared about was the price he had to pay after the fact.

To keep working for a woman who wanted to imprison these men and make the lives of anyone they cared about absolutely miserable.

"I'm sorry," Bill said. "I didn't want you to get hurt."

"You were with me for two years!"

She still wasn't over that part.

"And when I chose to leave her, I knew she'd look for a reason why. I couldn't be with you, or anyone, until I knew it was safe." Bill finally looked as though he was getting flustered.

"So what is this, then? Why did Esme throw us together, just for us to have to be ripped apart again when we go home?"

"Because... Lilly is no longer a threat to me." He took a deep breath. "A few months ago, someone hacked her system. Completely dismantled it. Now, my enhancements aren't connected to her tracking system anymore, and there are too many of us out there. Men she's enhanced. Men who hate her and who are no longer beholden to her and would hurt *her* if given the chance."

"*Months* ago?" Ray's jaw dropped. "*Months* ago, and you didn't come around sooner?"

"I never thought I had a chance to get you back." Bill looked down, taking her hand in his and staring at it like it was the most precious thing in the world.

Ray's head spun. She felt like she was being pulled toward him and pushed away at the same time.

She didn't like it, and she hated him for putting her in this position. "I am so fucking furious with you right now."

"I know."

"You could have told me something."

"Told you what?" Bill looked back up, meeting her fierce gaze with sad puppy-dog eyes. "That I was leaving you because my boss, the unhinged vampire, might come after you when I crossed her?"

"I would have waited for you!" Ray snapped, pulling her hand away so she could hold both of her temples as she shook her head.

Bill fell back a step, his eyes going wide.

He didn't say anything, and Ray wanted to cry.

Her throat closed up, and she was still so mad at him for doing this to her.

She felt wide open and raw, and she had no idea what to do with this horrible thing that was stuck inside her chest now.

Bill's eyes softened. "Baby."

Ray shook her head. Bill was blurry now. Her eyes were swimming, and she couldn't wipe them away fast enough. "I thought it was me. I thought I did something. That you didn't want me anymore, or I was too annoying or not smart enough."

"I never said that to you. I would never have said that to you because it's not true."

"You're always so serious," Ray said, and letting all this out, she knew it was true.

Bill was so tall and good-looking. He had the whole mysterious bodyguard thing down without a problem.

Meanwhile, Ray was a little loud, cute, but not the most

gorgeous woman—which Bill could easily pull. Sure, he laughed at some of her jokes, but half the time, she thought he was just placating her.

His job had seemed so important. He was a man in charge of keeping people safe. She'd had no idea who those people were or why they needed protecting. She'd thought maybe it was a celebrity type of thing, and he couldn't say who he worked for.

Looking back, she'd been so stupid, and it had bothered her to think that he might have believed that as well.

He did all of that, and she drew flowers and leaves and polka dots, selling them to companies to put on their toilet paper packages if she was lucky.

"If you'd just told me what was wrong... I would have waited for you. I thought it was because of me. Something I did."

"No, sweetheart, no," Bill went to her, folding her into his arms, and she let him.

She let him because she needed it.

She needed *him*.

No more pretending. No more lying to herself.

This was exactly what she needed.

"I missed you," she said.

Ray felt the press of Bill's lips in her hair. "I missed you, too. So much."

Ray clung to him. It was kind of pathetic, but fuck it. She needed this, and she wasn't going to say no to it now that she had it.

"Did that woman, Lilly, change your eyes?"

Bill sucked in a breath. "Yes. It was... it was just a job. At first. And then it was more like a prison."

"What's she like?" Ray asked. "Would she really have come after us?"

"Honestly, I thought I was safe," Bill said. "But I have a feeling there is more Dallas and Aaron aren't telling me. Your sister, Rita, stealing Bill right from under Lilly? No doubt Lilly has her sights set on getting revenge for that. And if I were a betting man, I'd say Aaron and Roquette might have something to do with Lilly's tracking and control database being destroyed, which means..."

"Lilly is targeting both of them." Ray nodded, absorbing the information. "So if I choose to be around them, I'll have to worry about Lilly too."

"Me too, because I'll be right at your side." Bill pressed his cheek to her head, holding her tightly.

"Really?"

"Yeah, really. This isn't what I expected when Esme offered me the cruise, but I... I missed you, and I was lonely."

Even though those weren't good feelings for him to have, Ray selfishly felt a rush of pleasure that he'd felt them at all.

He'd missed her.

He'd *missed* her.

Bill pulled back just enough to look her in the eyes, his big hands on her shoulder and cheek.

"I knew that if I left Lilly, I would have to leave you, too. I couldn't take you with me. I couldn't let her see that I'd left her to be with you... and I couldn't ask you to wait." He smiled wryly. "Am I the worst for feeling some relief about your sisters already being in Lilly's sights? Because now, I don't need to feel like I have to stay away to protect you..."

"Because I'm going to be around the danger anyway." Ray laughed a little. "No, you're not the worst at all. I'm more than glad for the excuse. Now you have nothing holding you back from being with me... if that's what you really want."

"I want you."

She pulled back a bit, looking into his eyes. "I used to think we were fated mates, but we'd never talked about it, never claimed each other."

He nodded. "Because I had Lilly to think about. I *couldn't* claim you."

"But you wanted to?"

"God, yes."

Ray pressed her lips together.

This was it. This was the answer she'd been dying for since the day he left her with that stupid text message.

Knowing it didn't ease the pain in her heart that it had happened.

She'd stupidly thought it would. That it would somehow make things better.

No, it didn't. The hurt was still there, but at least now she knew.

She knew it wasn't malicious. It wasn't because she'd done something wrong or because there was some flaw in herself that needed to be fixed.

It was a noble reason, honestly. He'd wanted to protect her.

"Did you really think I would never forgive you?"

He blinked at her. "I broke up with you over a text message."

She cringed. "Right, good point."

There was so much more she could ask. Part of her wanted to. Part of her wanted to go over every little detail and nitpick anything and everything that had happened.

When he realized he needed to leave. What exactly his job was. What sort of work had been done to him, and how much of it had he consented to? How long was he planning on leaving her before he finally did? What finally pushed him to contact Esme for help, and what would he do to make it up to Dallas?

Because knowing Bill, he was going to want to try.

"We should get those drinks and go back to your sisters," Bill said, his hands sliding up and down her arms. "I'm so proud of you. You found them."

"I didn't do anything," Ray muttered, pressing her forehead against Bill's solid wall of a chest. "Esme did."

"We'll send her a gift basket."

"We?"

She looked up at him. Bill's hands were suddenly off her arms, his expression unsure. "That is... if you would like me to... I would like to be there with you."

Ray swallowed hard. She reached for his hands, and she threaded their fingers together. "Yeah. I think I'd like that."

The smile on his face was pure relief. She'd never seen him look like that before.

"Thank you."

Ray still felt a whirl of emotions within her. She still felt high-strung and all over the place. Happy to have found her sisters at last. Grateful that Esme had been watching out for her. Thrilled that Bill was right here, holding her in his arms and telling her he wanted to be part of her life.

"So, are you gonna kiss me before we go and get those drinks? I think we're going to need them."

"Yeah," Bill laughed, sounding just as wrecked as she felt. "I get the feeling we're going to be doing a lot of talking with them. Catching up for you. Groveling for me."

Ray stroked her hands through Bill's hair, something she'd wanted to do from the first moment she saw him in her room on the ship. "I'll protect you. Don't worry."

She pulled him down for that kiss, holding him tightly, and knowing, for once, that things were going to get better now that they finally had each other.

The End.

...not quite!

There is still more to uncover! In the next book, the sisters and their mates will meet a long-lost aunt. "The Better Part of Valor" is a paranormal woman's fiction story with an older heroine as the main character!

And then in Book 5, "Etched in Brass," the sisters and their mates will finally face off with Lilly!

SHAPE UP OR SHIFT OUT SERIES

A Rose by Any Other Name
Winter of Discontent
Sea of Trouble
The Better Part of Valor
Etched in Brass

ABOUT THE AUTHOR

USA Today Bestselling Author Mandy Rosko is a videogame playing, book loving chick. She loves writing paranormal romances that range from light steamy to erotic, and has some contemporary and historical romances as well. You can find her on all sorts of platforms, including Twitch, where she does writing sprints, crafting, and video gaming!

Get all the latest news from Mandy by signing up for her newsletter: subscribepage.com/mandyroskobooks

As a bonus for signing up, you'll get her starter library, including Burns Like Fire, Sold to the Enemy, and The Vampire's Curse!

facebook.com/MandyRoskoRomance

instagram.com/mandyroskodraws

amazon.com/Mandy-Rosko/e/B008ETBVFW

bookbub.com/authors/mandy-rosko

goodreads.com/mandyrosko

youtube.com/UCD1z6r06dKoN-0WdUbi1pAQ

ALSO BY MANDY ROSKO

PARANORMAL ROMANCE

Blood Secrets

Darkness Awakened

Passion Awakened

Beauty Awakened (Coming Soon)

Eve Langlais' FUCN'A

I'll Be Dammed

Trash Queen

Chillin' Out

Bits and Bobs

Poisoned Kisses

Goddesses of Vengeance

Angel's Fury

Shape Up or Shift Out

A Rose by Any Other Name

Winter of Discontent

Sea of Trouble

The Better Part of Valor

Etched in Brass (Coming Soon)

Shifter Hospital

Alpha Medicine

Second Chance Alpha (Coming Soon)

The Aquaterrestrial Task Force

Get Kraken

Shark Bait

The Nightshade Guild

Mage to Disobey

Magic Confined

Defying Time

Crimson Moon Hideaway

(Amazon and KU Only)

Double Booked with Her Ex

Flame and Mist

Learn more at mandyrosko.com

www.ingramcontent.com/pod-product-compliance
Lightning Source LLC
Chambersburg PA
CBHW052051150726

48002CB00002B/848